I Got More Stories to Tell, Tale, Tail

Some Lies, Some Truths, Some Make Believe

I Got More Stories to Tell, Tale, Tail

Some Lies, Some Truths, Some Make Believe

---

*There's Always More Stories to Tell, Tale, Tail.
What's Your Story???*

A. Lee

Published by Creative Love Network Publishing
Los Angeles, CA
CreativeLoveNetwork.com

I Got More Stories to Tell, Tale, Tail: Some Lies, Some Truths, Some Make Believe
© 2026 A. Lee
ISBN: 978-1-961523-14-2 (paperback)
ISBN: 978-1-961523-16-6 (hardcover)
ISBN: 978-1-961523-15-9 (ebook)
Library of Congress Control Number: 2026912095

First Edition, 2026

To request permissions, you may contact the Publisher at
Info@CreativeLoveNetwork.com

Printed in the United States of America.

Cover design by A. Lee & Emily Anne Evans
Layout design by Emily Anne Evans
Edited by Maria Duarte

This book is dedicated to every version of me that didn't give up.
To the woman I was, the woman I am, and the woman I am still becoming.

To my children:
*you are my why, my heartbeat, my reason to keep going
even on the days I felt like I couldn't. Everything I build,
everything I create, is rooted in love for you.*

To my family and friends:
*thank you for your love, your support, your patience, and your belief in me.
You've held me up in ways you may never fully understand.*

To my community:
*to every voice, every story, every shared moment… thank
you for trusting me, for inspiring me, and for reminding me
that we are never alone in what we go through.*

To those who felt unseen, unheard, or misunderstood:
*this is for you. May these pages remind you that your story matters,
your voice is powerful, and your truth deserves to be told.*

And **to the ones we've lost, the pain we've
carried, and the lessons we've learned:**
you live within these pages.

**This book is more than words…
it is healing, truth, imagination, and growth.**

*With love, always—
Andrea Lee
(Ms. Drea The Poet).*

Contents

I Got More Stories to Tell, Tale, Tail

Some Lies, Some Truths, Some Make Believe

The Four Speak: Tell | Tale | Tail Whisper

Tell
(Water = Emotion)

I am the pulse beneath your skin. The quiet that hums between heartbeats. I move through memory like a river finding its own language. I am every tear you refused to let fall, every word that sat heavy on your tongue.

I do not ask for permission to flow. I am the mirror and the storm, the baptism and the drowning. I am what happens when you stop pretending to be strong long enough to remember that strength was never meant to be dry.

My lessons come softly at first, like drizzle on your shoulders. But if you ignore me, I come again harder, louder, unapologetic   until you listen. Because emotion is not weakness. It is the evidence that you are still here, still human, still alive enough to feel.

I carry stories that wash over pain and polish it into wisdom. I cleanse. I break open. I forgive. I am the body remembering how to release.

Call me when you are tired of holding it all. I will teach you how to let go without losing yourself. I am Tell—the water that feels everything and still dares to rise.

Tale
(Fire = Truth)

I am the voice that refuses to whisper. The spark that turns silence into sermon. I am the part of you that will not dim itself to make others comfortable.

I do not come to destroy; I come to reveal. My heat strips away illusions, leaving only what's real. I am truth with edges, love with boundaries, courage with scars.

I have lived in the throats of women who were told to hush, and in the hands of those who wrote their freedom into existence. I am the flame that carried Harriet through night, the fire in Zora's laughter, the glow in Audre's defiance.

I am not gentle, but I am necessary. To live without me is to live half-lit. You will learn that truth burns but the burn is how you know you're healing.

I am Tale—the fire that transforms every wound into wisdom, every ending into light.

Tail
(Earth = Root)

I am the ground that held you when the world turned its back. I am the soil beneath your stories the hum of your grandmother's prayers buried in my chest.

I know every name that was forgotten, every seed that never sprouted, everybody that learned how to bloom after being broken. I am patient, deliberate, ancient. I do not rush growth. I know it takes seasons to remember who you are.

I am the womb that carries your becoming. The dust that made you divine. I am the root that refused to rot.

Kneel if you must, not out of weakness but remembrance. Every time your knees hit the earth; you are closer to truth. I will show you how to build again how to plant yourself in purpose, how to trust your own roots.

I am Tail—the earth that grounds your grief and grows your glory.

Whisper
(Wind = Freedom)

I am the breath between stories. The whisper that moves mountains without a sound. I am the wind that carries your words to the next generation.

I live in movement in laughter that bursts open rooms, in the exhale that finally feels like peace. I cannot be owned, only felt. I have no color, no cage, no fear. I am what's left when you release everything else.

You will know me by the way your spirit rises for no reason. By the way your voice softens, and your faith sharpens. I am freedom in its purest form the invisible truth that touches everything and belongs to no one.

I have carried the scent of ancestors and the songs of children not yet born. I will not stop moving until every story finds its home.

I am Whisper—the wind that reminds you to breathe, to speak, to fly.

Together We Speak

We are the four that dwell in one.
Water feels. Fire reveals. Earth remembers. Wind releases.
And in our harmony, you will find her the woman who has lived
through every element, every silence, every storm, and still dares
to create.

I'm Learning to Move Like Water

I'm learning to move like water not rushing, not frozen, just aware
of every space I enter.

I no longer crash into walls, trying to prove my strength. I soften
first, then shape myself around what is hard.

I flow now.

Leaving behind names that no longer fit, releasing expectations
that were never mine to meet, outgrowing the pain that once tried
to contain me.

Water doesn't argue with stone. It learns it. Studies its edges. Wears
it down with patience, not force.

I'm learning that I don't have to be loud to be powerful. I don't have
to stay still to be grounded. I can change form and still be true.
Some days I am rain gentle, cleansing, falling exactly where I'm
needed.

Some days I am a river carrying memories, stories, and songs,
refusing to forget where I came from. And some days I am the
ocean vast, emotional, holding grief and joy in the same breath.

I'm learning to trust my tides. To pull back without guilt. To return
without apology. Because water survives everything fire, fracture,
time. It adapts. It remembers.

It keeps moving. And so do I. Like water love fills me up Keeps me full of love I'm learning to move like water, slowly, soft exploring being more gentle, loving.

I Am the Water That Remembers

Amelia always believed that water and wind were the only two things in her life that told the truth. Water remembered everything she tried to forget, and wind carried everything she didn't yet have the courage to say. She felt it the moment she woke each morning that subtle tremor inside her chest, like a tide pulling at her bones, whispering pieces of stories she never meant to inherit. *I am the water that remembers*, she thought, not fully understanding why the words felt like an ache lodged beneath her ribs. The truth was that she had been carrying her grandmother's voice long before she understood words, a gentle current that ran through her bloodline, shaping her in ways she didn't yet have a name for.

Wind rattled the bedroom window that morning, brushing over her skin like a warning, tugging strands of her hair as if urging her to listen. Wind had always been the messenger in her life unpredictable, shifting, honest the one element that refused to let silence breed lies. As a child, she used to sit outside on the back steps of their old Los Angeles apartment while the Santa Ana winds howled through the alleyways like restless spirits. She remembered hugging her knees to her chest, her young body tight with fear, wondering why the wind always sounded angry. *Maybe it's trying to carry someone away*, she used to think. *Maybe it's trying to carry me.*

Younger Amelia didn't have the language for trauma, but she felt it like a bruise stitched into her heartbeat, like a storm she didn't know how to outrun. She felt it every time her mother flinched at footsteps, every time her father's voice cracked like thunder through the house, every time she and her twin pressed their backs together in the dark, trying to breathe past fear. Wind would slip through the cracks under the door, swirling around her toes, whispering *hold on, little girl, hold on*. She didn't know if it was comforting her or warning her, but she listened, because wind never lied.

Now grown, she felt that same wind brushing against her skin not angry, but insistent urging her to face the memories water had always held for her. *The current that carried her grandmother's voice across generations,* she murmured internally. She could hear that voice now, soft but heavy, wrapped in sadness that never found freedom. Her mother never healed, never screamed, never allowed the wind to take away the weight she carried. Instead, she drowned quietly, her pain sinking into Amelia the way water seeps into the earth, unnoticed but irreversible.

As Amelia thought of her younger self small, wide-eyed, trembling she felt water rise inside her chest. Not tears, but memory. *The soft flood that drowned her fears before she could name them.* She remembered being five years old, sitting beside the bathtub watching her mother scrub her arms so hard the skin turned red. "I'm washing the day off me," her mother whispered, her voice thin and defeated. At that age, Amelia wondered if she could scrub off her fear too the fear of yelling, of hands grabbing, of footsteps down the hall. She wished the wind would pick her up and carry her somewhere safe, somewhere she didn't have to be so small and so brave at the same time.

Water remembered everything she wished it would release.

Even now, as an adult, she spoke in waves sometimes gentle, sometimes crashing depending on who stood before her. When she loved, she loved like calm tide pools: steady, soothing, dependable. When she was hurt, she became rip currents: sharp, sudden, dragging truths to the surface that she had tried to bury. Wind danced around her then, swirling her words through the air, making her honesty feel like confession. She hated and loved that about herself her inability to hide the storm inside her.

But there were moments when she felt cleansing rise in her spirit, moments where the wind inside her chest grew strong enough to push out the weight of what she'd carried for years. In those moments she understood the purpose of both elements: wind moved what water remembered. Wind swept away what she didn't need to hold anymore. Wind shook loose the pieces of her heart that grew mold in silence. Wind scattered the ghosts. Wind said *no more* in a voice she tried for years to find on her own.

Standing near the window now, she felt the breeze shift soft at first, then insistent lifting the hair from her shoulders as though urging her to let go of the stories that had drowned her since childhood.

I cleanse what cannot stay, **she whispered to herself.**

And for the first time in a long time, she felt something loosen inside her.

Something heavy.
Something old.
Something she no longer needed to carry.
Because she finally understood:
She was not only the water that remembered
she was also the wind that released.
And both were hers to command.

"I wasn't raised with love.
I was raised with survival."

Love Is My Religion

Love is my religion
not the soft, pastel kind
they preach about from pulpits
while hiding their sins behind stained glass,
but the gritty kind
the kind born from blood, bruises,
and a thousand silent prayers
no one ever heard but God.

Love is my religion
because pain tried to convert me
into something bitter,
something empty,
something unrecognizable
and still,
my heart rose up
like scripture rewritten in my own handwriting.

I learned my worship in the dark.
On nights my breath felt like broken glass.
On days my name sounded foreign to my own ears.
On mornings I held my reflection like a stranger
and whispered,
"Come back. Don't leave me too."

Love is my religion
because survival wasn't enough for me
I wanted resurrection.
I wanted to rise hungry for joy,
not haunted by memory.
I wanted to feel the holiness
in my own heartbeat
after years of believing it was unworthy
of praise.

Love became my altar
when the world became unkind.
My tears became baptism
when no one reached out their hands.
My voice became a psalm
when silence tried to choke me.
I became my own sanctuary
because no one built one for me.

Love is my religion
because it demands participation
not perfection.
Because it asks me to show up
when fear tells me to fold.
Because it teaches me to worship truth,
to kneel only to growth,
to bow only to the God within me
that refused to die.

And every day I practice devotion
not to another soul,
but to the woman who crawled through hell
and still remembered how to love.
Deep.
Messy.
All-consuming.
Healing.
Rebellious.
Real.

Love is my religion
because nothing else saved me.
Nothing else made me whole.
Nothing else felt more like home
than the moment I decided
finally, fiercely,
unapologetically
to love myself first.

Look inward and
discover
Self-Love

Born & Raised
Every Block Taught Her Something—Love Wasn't One of Them

Amelia was all parts of Los Angeles.

She didn't just grow up in the city she *carried* it, every street and neighborhood stitched into her bones like a living map. She was born at Los Angeles Hospital off Western near the 10 freeway, and from the moment she arrived, stability was never something she knew. Her mother moved them constantly every year, sometimes twice dragging her across the entire city: Watts, Compton, Long Beach, Crenshaw, Inglewood, Baldwin Hills. New apartments, new neighbors, new schools, new dangers.

Each neighborhood gave her culture diversity, rhythm, language, food, community, color
but none of them ever gave her safety or love.

School was a revolving door of trauma. Amelia never remembered much from her earliest years. Her childhood existed inside a fog blurred, fragmented, and scattered like someone had taken scissors to her memories and removed the parts that hurt too deeply to relive. She couldn't recall teachers' faces, her elementary school classrooms, or the sound of her own young handwriting. What she remembered instead were the pictures school photos with stiff collars, tight forced smiles, and generic backdrops. Those photos were proof she had been there, even when her memory refused to hold anything else.

But between the confusion and trauma, there was one bright, undamaged period a time that stood out with color and warmth: the months she spent living with her grandmother after social services removed her and her siblings from their mother's care. Those were the only memories that felt safe and whole. Her grandmother's home smelled like warm cornbread and Vaseline. It felt steady in a way nothing else in her life ever had. She woke Amelia with soft calls from the kitchen "Rise and shine, baby girl, breakfast is ready." A voice free from anger, a tone free from chaos. When Amelia entered the kitchen, her grandmother always smiled, asking gently, "You slept good?" And when Amelia nodded, her grandmother would say, "Mm-hmm. Peace look good on you." Those mornings were filled with tenderness. Her grandmother brushed her hair before school, firm but gentle, telling her, "Hold still, baby. This tender-headedness ain't gon' stop me from making you look decent." Then she would kiss her forehead and send her off with: "Go on learn something today."

Those school days were the only ones Amelia remembered clearly. Her grandmother attended every event every play, assembly, and open house clapping for Amelia even when she didn't win anything. "That's my baby right there!" she'd shout proudly, her joy filling the room. After school one day, Amelia handed her grandmother a picture she drew two stick figures with a red heart between them. "What's this?" her grandmother asked. "Us, Grandma," Amelia replied. Her grandmother's eyes softened instantly. "Baby, you don't know how much that means to me. You made my whole day." She pulled Amelia into a hug that smelled of baby powder and peppermint, anchoring her to a feeling she wouldn't experience again for years. Those days were filled with three meals, warm beds, steady routines, and love that expected nothing from her except to simply be a child.

But everything changed the day social services decided she and her siblings would be returned to their abusive mother. Amelia remembered the social workers standing stiffly in her grandmother's living room, holding clipboards and wearing smiles that never reached their eyes. "We believe reunification is in the best interest of the children," one of them declared. Amelia didn't understand the words, but she recognized the fear in her grandmother's face. Her grandmother knelt in front of her and held her hands tightly. "Listen to me, baby girl. You remember everything I taught you, okay? You remember that you're loved. You remember that you are somebody." Tears welled in Amelia's eyes as she whispered, "Grandma... I don't wanna go." Her grandmother pulled her into her arms, hugging her as if she could protect her from the world. "I know, sweetheart. I know. If I could keep you, I would. God knows I would." A single tear ran down her grandmother's cheek the first time Amelia had ever seen her cry. When the social worker cleared her throat and said, "It's time," her grandmother squeezed tighter, whispering, "No matter where they take you, my love goes with you. You understand me?" Amelia nodded into her shoulder. "I love you, Grandma." "I love you more. Always."

Her grandmother's love wasn't enough to stop the system.

And from that day forward, Amelia learned what it meant to be failed repeatedly by child welfare, by the courts, by adults who never protected her or her siblings. When she returned to her mother's house, stability vanished instantly. The yelling, chaos, and violence returned like they had never left. They moved every year, usually around the holidays. Thanksgiving or Christmas, her mother would pack up the house and say, "This is your Christmas present," dumping bags onto the floor of yet another unfamiliar apartment. There were no traditions, no roots, no consistency just constant uprooting.

Those good memories with her grandmother became her anchor. In the darkest moments of her childhood, Amelia held onto her grandmother's voice, her hands brushing her hair, her cheers in crowded school auditoriums, her warm hugs. Those memories reminded her that safety had existed, even if it was temporary. They reminded her she was worth loving, even if the world around her didn't show it. They became the one stable part of an unstable life. And long after the system failed her, long after the moves, the fights, the storms, and the trauma, Amelia carried her grandmother's love inside her. It was the one place she ever truly felt at home and the only reason she survived. Returning to her mother's house was never a homecoming—it was a sentence. Her mother's house had no warmth, no routine, no structure. It shifted from moment to moment, unpredictable and unstable, like living inside a storm that never passed. The only thing that remained the same were the beatings and the mistreatment. There was no protection, no hugs, barely any food, and never any love. School became one of the few places she was required to go, but it was not a refuge. After leaving her grandmother's care, Amelia attended Carver Elementary, and everything after that became a blur. The constant moving made every school, every street, every face blend into one long memory of survival.

Growing up felt like walking through a storm she never asked to enter. Her body remembered things her mind refused to speak on the danger, the fear, the yelling, the threats, and the homes that felt sharp, as if the walls themselves had teeth. So much of her childhood was erased by trauma, leaving shadows where memories should have been. But one part of her childhood remained clear: Willowbrook Middle School in Watts, California. She remembered the tan buildings, the cracked blacktop where kids played or argued, and the smell of cafeteria burritos drifting through the hallways. She lived off 126th and Wilmington, close enough to walk, though she had to watch her surroundings with every step.

In middle school, Amelia kept quiet. She didn't know how to make long-term friends because her life had never taught her stability. She knew how to smile politely, how to disappear into corners, how to blend into rooms without being noticed. Kids welcomed her into their circles for a week or two, but friendships never lasted long enough to grow roots. Sometimes, the wrong kids gravitated toward her the loud ones, the angry ones, the ones who fought because fighting was the only language they knew. Amelia wasn't a fighter; she was the in-between girl, the peacemaker, the one trying to keep different storms from colliding, even as lightning struck inside her own home. Still, trouble always found her fights, bullying, and chaos she didn't ask to be part of.

She remembered one particular girl a new student with beautiful, long wavy hair that glistened in the sun. She looked like she belonged to a world far from 126th Street. But one girl in their friend group disliked her immediately. Whether it was jealousy, insecurity, or simply the way kids learned to survive by attacking first, she began teasing the new girl relentlessly. "Your hair fake." "You think you cute." "I'ma beat you up after school." Day after day, the insults and threats continued. The new girl had no one to defend her and nowhere to hide. Months later, she came back to school with her entire head shaved. Amelia remembered feeling her breath catch, her stomach sinking as she looked at the girl who had changed her whole identity because someone else controlled her fear. She couldn't understand how another child could hold so much power over someone's spirit. Now, she knew. Trauma makes you adjust yourself to survive. It teaches you to shrink, to silence yourself, to disappear in hopes the danger will disappear too.

Amelia stayed at Willowbrook maybe one semester, maybe two. What she remembered most was the packing the boxes, the black trash bags used as suitcases, the constant movement. Moving was always chaos. While other kids decorated trees or ate holiday meals with family, Amelia learned new bus routes, new neighborhoods, new threats. Every year felt like starting over: new school, new apartment, new faces, no friendships, no safety. Stability was something she saw only in movies, never in her own life. This became her pattern a childhood defined by carrying broken pieces from one zip code to the next, learning to adjust, adapt, and survive. Through all of that movement and instability, one truth remained: Amelia was still here. And that alone proved her strength.

After Willowbrook, they moved again. This time to Los Angeles off Western and 75th, where she attended Horseman Middle School for one semester. Then another move after that, they moved once more to 65th and Vermont, between Gage and Vermont. Onto John Muir Middle School. And this was where the trauma grew darker, heavier, and sharper.

Growing up felt like surviving a storm she never asked to walk into. Her body held memories her mind refused to speak on the danger, the yelling, the threats, the unpredictability, the homes that felt sharp and crowded with fear. Trauma blocked out most of her childhood, leaving only shadows where memories should have been. But one part of her childhood remained painfully clear: moved every year. Amelia learned new bus routes, new neighborhoods, new threats. Each year felt like starting over: new school, new apartment, new faces. No friendships. No safety. No stability. And that became her life a childhood spent carrying broken pieces across zip codes, learning to adjust and survive. Yet through all of it, one truth remained: Amelia was still here, and her survival made her stronger than she realized. After she and her siblings were returned to their mother's care and Amelia finished middle school, the cycle of uprooting continued. We moved again, this time to Compton, I enrolled at Centennial High School. Another school, another set of hallways, another place I didn't choose. I walked through those doors carrying every piece of the life she survived, not yet knowing that this next chapter would test her strength in ways she never could have imagined.

•••

Amelia attended Centennial High School for two days before witnessing someone get stabbed in the hallway. Then came Susan Miller Dorsey Senior High School, where tension lived in the air like humidity. On her first week, after the final bell rang, gunshots cracked near the front gate. A wave of screaming students ran past her, pushing her to the ground as someone collapsed on the sidewalk. Amelia didn't breathe until she got home.

Amelia's mother moved again, and she ended up at Dominguez High School, where violence shadowed the campus like a cloud. Fights, threats, police cars, lockdowns it was all routine.

By the time Amelia reached adulthood She had survived more trauma than most people confess in a lifetime. Everywhere she went, she learned to read danger faster than she could read textbooks.

And home didn't offer shelter from anything.
Inside those walls, love didn't live there.
Affection wasn't spoken.
Hugs didn't exist.
Protection was mythical something she saw in movies
but never felt in real life.
Her mother withheld softness like punishment. She believed love made children weak.

Her father's presence swayed between charm and cruelty, leaving Amelia confused about what love was supposed to feel like. Whether she was physically gone or emotionally absent, she was always left reaching for something that never reached back.

The Streets of Los Angeles Raised Me

The streets of Los Angeles raised me. I was dealt a bad hand not one good parent to nurture me, not one gentle voice to say those three words I love you.

No one protected me from anything. I was used like a punching bag, treated like a slave clean everything, fix everything, stay quiet, stay small.

School wasn't a priority. Survival was.

One parent chose drugs over their children, powder and needles before protection. The other chose religion without compassion scripture without shelter, rules without rescue.

By seven years old I was already walking alone, too young for the weight of the night, moving through late streets where innocence disappears early and fear learns your name.

It was nothing but God and the streets of LA that raised me. Streetlights became prayers. Sirens sang lullabies. Concrete caught my tears when no arms ever did.

But the libraries saved me. Once I picked up a book, I got lost in words. My imagination became my escape pages opened doors that my life kept locked.

The words shaped visions of a better life, a better future, somewhere beyond what I was living. Time floated when I read. Reality softened. Books helped me save myself from the truth of a life no child should ever have to resign to.

I began writing my story in the form of poetry, short books, quiet truths. I hid them all inside because I was too ashamed to let anyone know what was really happening inside a home that was never built for children. As I got older, my pride swallowed me whole. I kept the pattern alive not asking for help, doing it alone, carrying everything by myself.

But I always found freedom in books. In writing. In words that let me breathe. The library was always open to me when nothing else was.

No judgment.

No questions.

Just space to exist, to dream, to heal quietly. There's a reason I'm still here. I am a walking testament. Breathing proof. Faith stitched me together when everything else tried to break me. Even when I didn't believe, something believed in me. Someone something was always watching over me.

So now I write. And now I share. These words are my testimony. For the child I was. For the streets that didn't kill me. For the libraries that saved me. And for the life I was never supposed to have but claimed anyway.

No Love
She Learned to Be Quiet Before She Learned to Be Safe

Amelia grew up not knowing love
only the shadows it left behind.
She learned to stay quiet, stay small, stay alert.
She learned to soothe adults who should've been soothing her
She learned to brace herself before storms, before yelling,
before the sound of doors slamming.
Trauma trained her before life did.
Yet despite it all, she grew into brilliance.
She became tall, intelligent, intuitive a woman with a presence that filled rooms without trying she became a writer whose pain became poetry, a chef who cooked comfort she never received, a therapist-in-training who learned to heal others long before she learned to heal herself.

Most people loved her instantly.
Not because they knew new her…

but because they felt her

Still when it came to love, her childhood lingered like smoke. Amelia kept choosing men who mirrored her parents: inconsistent, distant, manipulative, emotionally unavailable, sometimes dangerous. They mistook her softness for weakness and her empathy for permission. She accepted breadcrumbs because she had grown up starving.

But something in her had begun to shift.

She wanted peace.

She wanted healing.

She wanted the kind of love she had never seen modeled not even once.

And tonight, in the middle of Leimert Park, that shift bloomed.

It was a cool Friday night outside Hot & Cool Café, the kind of night that feels charged with possibility. The drum circle echoed from the plaza, scents of incense and roasted corn drifting through the air. People gathered in clusters artists, poets, community elders, teenagers with notebooks each person a story waiting to be heard.

Amelia sat on the curb, notebook open on her lap, pen tapping rhythmically as she wrote the truth she'd avoided for years:

"I wasn't raised with love.

But I am determined to learn it anyway."

She read it twice, feeling her heart press against her chest.

"You write like you hiding something," a voice said.

She looked up.

A man stood a few feet away Kingston Black. Tall. Strong. Tattoos running down his forearms like prayers written in ink. His eyes held a quiet storm, something wounded but controlled. He had a sketchbook in his hand, and Amelia realized he'd been drawing her.

His gaze wasn't invasive it was knowing. Like he recognized pain the way a survivor recognizes another survivor.

She didn't know yet that Kingston would become the fire of her story the part that burns and transforms.

Before she could respond, another voice called her name from behind.

Zora Mayfield approached in her EMT uniform, her curly hair pulled into a messy bun, the energy around her sharp but warm. Zora had the presence of someone who ran into danger for a living and still kept her humor intact. She had come to support her cousin Shaq at the open mic, but the moment she saw Amelia, her eyes softened with curiosity as if sensing a connection neither of them could explain yet.

Zora would become the fire of the story
the unexpected twist,
the truth hidden in shadow,
the woman whose path would collide with Amelia's
in life-changing ways.

Amelia's name was called for the mic.

She stood up slowly, notebook pressed to her chest. Her palms were sweating not from fear, but from the weight of finally speaking the truth she'd carried for decades.

The crowd quieted as she stepped onto the small stage.
Kingston leaned against the wall, eyes fixed on her.
Zora crossed her arms, studying her like a puzzle piece she wasn't ready to place yet.

Amelia inhaled deeply and let her truth pour out:
"I wasn't raised with love.
But I deserve it.
And tonight...
I'm choosing myself."
The room stilled.
And in that moment
the universe shifted.
Her healing began.
And all three of their stories silently intertwined.

Now Get Ready:
You're About to Become a Character

Before you turn this page, before you decide this is just another book, understand this: this is not a story you observe from a safe distance. This is not a lean back and watch kind of read. This is a step inside kind of book. If you are looking for clean endings, heroes without flaws, or pain that stays neatly on the page, you may want to pause right now. Because once you begin, you are no longer just the reader. You become the witness, the stand-by, the voice someone didn't have on the day everything fell apart. In just a moment, you become a character in the story of someone's worst day ever not because you caused it or deserved it, but because life has a way of pulling us into moments that change how we see ourselves, how we see others, and how we understand survival.

These stories are not polished for comfort. They are told the way life hands them to us unfinished, breathless, sometimes cruel, sometimes beautiful, often both at the same time. Some of what you will read is truth. Some of it is fiction dressed up just enough to survive being told. Some of it is a lie that feels familiar because it mirrors something you lived through but never named out loud. You will meet characters who love too hard, leave too late, stay when they should run, run when they should stay, and discover that the most dangerous place to be is inside your own head on the day everything finally collapses.

Somewhere between the lines, between the tale and the tail, between what is spoken and what is swallowed, you may recognize yourself your voice, your silence, your survival. This book is for those who kept going after the worst phone call, the longest night, the moment that split life into before and after. It is for those who learned that healing does not move in straight lines and that stories do not always end where we want them to.

So, take a breath. Bring your honesty. Leave your armor at the door. Because once you turn the page, you are not just reading a story you are walking into someone's worst moments and discovering what it takes to live through it. Welcome to the story. You are already in it.

Your voice.
Your silence.
Your survival.

Welcome to *I Got More Stories to Tell, Tale, Tail...*
(Water-Fire-Earth-Wind)
You're already in it.

PART ONE - TELL (WATER)

———

Born into the Flood

*Before She Could Speak, the Storm
Already Knew Her Name*

Amelia Stevenson entered the world like a raindrop falling into a storm unwanted, unprotected, and unprepared. Born in the summer heat of Los Angeles in 1977, twin to her sister and fourth of seven children, she arrived in a house already drowning in chaos. Even before she could speak, she sensed the tension in the walls, the heaviness in the air, and the way her mother Patricia born Amanda Duns used God's name like a weapon. In that house, everything was the devil except the real demons walking freely. Patricia hid behind religion while delivering punishments more faithfully than any prayer. Her hands struck quicker than her words. Her voice cut deeper than any belt.

As a child, Amelia often thought, *"Here goes this bitch again. I hate her."* She prayed constantly, begging God to explain why she had been born into this family. Why this life. Why this pain. But no answer came only survival. *"My mother hates me,"* she would whisper into the dark, too embarrassed to tell anyone what was happening. She tried to earn Patricia's love cleaning more, staying silent, forcing smiles but the harder she tried, the more Patricia singled her out. While her siblings were treated like gold and praised for the smallest things, Amelia was starved, beaten, belittled, and ignored. Her siblings pretended they were a normal family, but it was all for show. They didn't feel her pain, so they didn't acknowledge it. And so, she carried everything alone fear, shame, hunger, confusion bottled inside her small, breaking body.

Her father Tyler Smith was no savior, no softness, no opposite to Patricia's cruelty. He moved in and out of state penitentiaries, drowning himself in drugs and alcohol and unleashing violence on anyone who crossed him. Amelia barely knew him, but the little she did know was enough to mark her forever. The fall of 1991 etched itself into her memory. Walking home from school that day, she felt a heaviness she couldn't explain, as if something terrible was hiding behind the front door waiting to strike. When she walked inside, she heard a man's voice she didn't recognize. Patricia turned and said sharply, "Your dad's home. He's going to be living with us now." A wave of disgust rippled through Amelia, though she didn't understand why.

For a month straight, arguments filled the house explosions behind closed doors, accusations shouted through thin walls. One night, Amelia heard her father yelling, "Why didn't you change her last name if she's, my child?" Patricia's voice trembled as she answered, "I didn't have time or money. You know I've only been with you." A slap echoed through the hall, followed by her mother's pleading. Days later, Tyler returned with flowers and mumbled apologies. For a brief moment, the house pretended to be normal. They even ate dinner together as a family something they had never done before. Amelia felt a flicker of warmth, a rare softness she wished she could believe in.

But illusions shatter quickly in houses like theirs.

One evening, while the family sat at the dinner table laughing, Tyler made a comment about Amelia never amounting to anything. Before she could process the insult, the room blacked out. When she opened her eyes, she was on the dining room floor, her sisters screaming above her, her head pounding, blood warm on her face. Tyler stood over her, reached his hand out as if to help, then sneered, "You little hoe-ass bitch. I bet you won't roll your eyes at me again." He walked away, leaving her bleeding and humiliated. She crawled to the bathroom, stared at her reflection, and hardly recognized the swollen, blood-streaked girl staring back. "Why me, God?" she whispered. There was no answer only pain.

The next morning, Patricia handed her the script: "Tell them you got in a fight at school. If you say anything else, they'll take the other kids, and I won't get any money. Don't be selfish." Not a question about her pain. Not a glance at her face. Not a moment of motherhood. Just manipulation. Just warning. Just Patricia.

The violence escalated. One night, Tyler snapped fists first, then feet, then a wooden stick handed to him silently by Patricia. That betrayal hurt more than the blows. Amelia saw a sliver of freedom in the cracked front door and ran for her life, tunnel vision blurring the world around her. She fled to her best friend Shelby's home, praying she was there. Shelby opened the door, shocked and horrified by Amelia's beaten face and trembling body. The girls cried together. Shelby hid her for a week until her mother rarely home due to working two jobs found out. Once they explained everything, Shelby's mom contacted the police.

Two officers arrived, took their statements, and transported Amelia to the 77th Police Station in Los Angeles. A female officer questioned her gently, photographed every bruise, every cut, every welt. When the officer called Patricia to inform her, Patricia asked to speak to Amelia. Over the phone, her mother didn't ask if she was hurt. She didn't ask if she was safe. Instead, she said, "Just tell them you made it up. Say some kids jumped you. If you don't, they'll take the others, and I won't get any money. Don't be selfish." Same script. Amelia dropped the phone and sobbed until she couldn't breathe.

She was placed into foster care. Eventually, when Patricia refused to leave Tyler, the other children were removed as well. Only then did Patricia act like she cared got a job, attended meetings, played the role long enough to get her children back. Amelia returned home, but nothing was different. The beatings resumed. The blame returned. Patricia's obsession with cleanliness, control, and cruelty grew heavier. She would beat Amelia for anything breathing too loud, cleaning too slow, speaking too softly. "You're stupid. You'll never be anything," she hissed daily. And if Amelia mumbled a word under her breath, Patricia stormed in, dragged her from bed, and beat her until her eyes swelled shut.

One night, after another beating, Amelia waited until the entire house was asleep. She packed nothing there was nothing to pack and slipped silently out the door. She didn't know where she was going. She only knew she couldn't stay. And as she stepped into the night, WIND brushed past her cheek like a whisper, a reminder that even water finds a way to move.

And so, she ran. Not away from home, but toward her life.

•••

Amelia recalled a night when she was around eight or nine years of age. Her mom had a guy friend that they called Godfather; he used to come in her room at night and molest her. Amelia was confused she told her older sister, and she told Amelia the same thing had happened to her and not to say anything because their mom would be upset. So, Amelia told her grandmother, who confronted their mother about the situation. Patricia, of course, took his side. Her reply to the whole situation was, "He has me; why would he want a child?" Patricia called Amelia a liar and stated that she wasn't ruining her life. "I don't know why I had you. I knew that you were a mistake from the beginning. You ran off Tyler, and I refuse to let you run him off, you little lying hoe bitch." Amelia tried to love her mother. Amelia thought to herself why couldn't she just love me back? Amelia couldn't figure out why her mom didn't love her like she loved the others. Amelia would try to hug and kiss her; she would push Amelia away and call one of her brothers or sisters over and hug and kiss them, then look at Amelia and smile. Patricia attempted to give Amelia away on several occasions; she even paid a man to take me away. As Amelia got older, she would ask her why she didn't love me or show me any affection and why she allowed so many bad things to happen to me. Her response was, "I don't recall." Amelia eventually tried to look for love in other places. She started dressing provocatively, hanging with loose older females, trying to fit in wherever she could. She ended up in several bad situations. The girls that Amelia was hanging out with dared her to sneak over to a guy's house with them. she agreed. Amelia arrived at a dark building. A guy appeared; she started to become afraid. He assured her there was nothing to worry about and that her friends were inside. Against her will, She was forced inside. Amelia heard cries for help, a gun went off, and it was silent from then on. The guy that forced Amelia inside said, "Now do what you're told or the same thing will happen to you. Your fate is in your hands. Now take off your clothes and don't make me ask twice. "Amelia was brutally raped that night repeatedly for several hours. The next day She was released with a threat that if she told anyone, she would die. Amelia went home and took a long shower. Even though She believed the threat was real, Amelia told her mother, thinking that she would sympathize and love her. Amelia was wrong. Patricia smirked and replied, "I knew you were a hoe and everything that happened to you, you deserved." Her mother was a cold piece of work. Her own mother, can you imagine that? Amelia's life just went downhill from there.

Something inside Amelia shifted. She didn't feel like a child anymore. She didn't feel safe in her own skin. Amelia didn't trust anyone not adults, not girls her age, not family, not even herself. Amelia walked around with this silent rage inside of her, mixed with shame and confusion. Every time Amelia looked at her mother, she wondered how a woman could carry a child for nine months, give birth to her, and still feel nothing. It was like she hated the very air Amelia breathed. She looked at me like I was the worst mistake she ever made, like Amelia owed her for existing.

The days after the assault felt like a blur. Amelia remembers going to school pretending everything was fine, sitting in class with this heavy secret inside her. No one knew that last night Amelia had begged God to just let me disappear. She remembers teachers asking her if she was okay and Amelia lying through her teeth, saying I was just tired. Amelia had learned early on that telling the truth in her family only made life worse. Silence became her shield.

Every time Amelia passed a mirror, she barely recognized herself. Her eyes looked older. Her body felt foreign. She felt dirty, haunted, and used up before she ever had the chance to learn who she was. And every time she thought about telling someone else, she heard his voice threatening her, and then Amelia heard her mother's voice telling She deserved it. Between the two of them, fear won.

At night, Amelia cried quietly into her pillow, so no one could hear her. Crying wasn't allowed in the house; tears only brought more trouble. Amelia felt trapped in a cycle She couldn't break violence outside the house, violence inside the house, no safe place for her anywhere. She didn't know who to turn to. She didn't know how to heal. She didn't even know healing was possible.

So, Amelia started closing herself off. I stopped caring about school, stopped hoping for a better future, stopped dreaming. She became numb. And numbness became the only way Amelia could survive.

Stillness once frightened Amelia because silence used to mean danger. It meant waiting. Watching. Bracing for what might come next. In her early life, quiet was never peaceful; it was loaded, heavy with uncertainty. So, she learned to fill space with noise, movement, survival. Stillness felt like exposure.

But healing changed the sound of silence.

Now, in quiet moments, she found comfort instead of fear. Early mornings became sacred no demands, no explanations, just breath and presence. In still waters, she began to hear what had always been there beneath the noise: her intuition, steady and sure, rising gently to the surface.

You deserve more.

You deserve softness.

You deserve love that doesn't make you shrink.

The words didn't shout. They didn't rush her. They arrived calmly, like ripples spreading across glassy water. For the first time, she trusted them. She let them settle into her bones, rewriting truths she had learned too young and too harshly.

Amelia didn't know it yet, but one day a man named Terrance would speak those same truths aloud not as a savior, not as a rescuer, but as a mirror. Someone who would see her clearly and confirm what the still waters had already told her: that she was worthy of love that felt safe, expansive, and true.

Life moved in tides rising and falling, giving and taking, pulling her forward and then back again. Amelia began to notice the pattern once she stopped resisting it. Every emotion, every season, every loss and return had its own timing. Nothing stayed high forever. Nothing stayed low forever. The tide always turned.

She learned to ride the waves instead of fighting them. Fighting had exhausted her left her gasping, angry at the water for doing what water does. So, she softened. She listened. She let herself move with what was happening instead of bracing against it. In that surrender, something shifted.

She stopped apologizing for her emotions, recognizing they were not inconveniences but signals messages from within asking to be honored. She stopped minimizing her pain, no longer shrinking her truth to make others comfortable. Her feelings were not too much; they were honest.

The tides taught her rhythm. They showed her when to advance and when to rest, when to speak and when to be still. Amelia realized the waves were never trying to drown her they were teaching her how to move with life, how to trust her own timing, how to stay standing even as the water rose around her.

Forgiveness was a pool Amelia feared stepping into. She stood at its edge for years, staring at the surface, convinced it was too deep, too cold, too dangerous. Forgiving her parents felt impossible—*how do you forgive people who never taught you love, who were supposed to protect you but became the wound?* The question lived in her chest like a locked door.

For a long time, she believed forgiveness meant excusing the harm, erasing the truth, pretending it didn't happen. But healing taught her otherwise. Forgiveness wasn't about rewriting the past or absolving anyone of responsibility. It wasn't about them at all. It was about freeing herself from carrying pain that no longer served her.

When she finally stepped in, it wasn't all at once. One foot. A pause. A breath. The water surprised her warm, steady, patient. Each step felt like stepping into relief after a lifetime of cold rain, the kind that soaks you to the bone and convinces you warmth is a myth. In this pool, she didn't forget what happened; she released the grip it had on her present.

Forgiveness didn't make her weak it made her lighter. And as the water reached her waist, then her heart, Amelia realized she wasn't drowning. She was buoyant. Held. Choosing herself.

Rain Check

She started saying no not with guilt,
not with long explanations, but with clarity.
No to overextending herself.
No to being available when her spirit felt empty.
No to carrying what was never hers to hold.
She started choosing **rest over rushing**, understanding that exhaustion was not a badge of honor and busyness was not proof of worth. The world had taught her to stay moving, to keep surviving, but healing asked her to pause. To listen. To breathe.

She began canceling plans that drained her, honoring her body when it whispered instead of waiting until it screamed. Each "maybe another day" felt like reclaiming a piece of herself that had been given away too easily for too long.

A **rain check** became an act of self-love intentional, necessary, sacred. Like rain, it slowed everything down. It softened the ground beneath her feet. It gave her time to breathe, to replenish, to remember that she was allowed to choose herself without apology.

The Pool of Forgiveness

Forgiveness was a pool she feared stepping into. Forgiving her parents felt impossible for years how do you forgive people who never taught you love? But forgiveness wasn't for them. It was for her. Each step into that pool felt like stepping into warm water after a lifetime of cold rain.

Forgiveness was a pool Amelia feared stepping into. She stood at its edge for years, staring at the surface, convinced it was too deep, too cold, too dangerous. Forgiving her parents felt impossible *how do you forgive people who never taught you love, who were supposed to protect you but became the wound?* The question lived in her chest like a locked door.

For a long time, she believed forgiveness meant excusing the harm, erasing the truth, pretending it didn't happen. But healing taught her otherwise. Forgiveness wasn't about rewriting the past or absolving anyone of responsibility. It wasn't about them at all. It was about freeing herself from carrying pain that no longer served her.

When she finally stepped in, it wasn't all at once. One foot. A pause. A breath. The water surprised her warm, steady, patient. Each step felt like stepping into relief after a lifetime of cold rain, the kind that soaks you to the bone and convinces you warmth is a myth. In this pool, she didn't forget what happened; she released the grip it had on her present.

Forgiveness didn't make her weak it made her lighter. And as the water reached her waist, then her heart, Amelia realized she wasn't drowning. She was buoyant. Held. Choosing herself.

Tides Life moved in tides rising and falling, giving and taking. Amelia learned to ride the waves instead of fighting them. She stopped apologizing for her emotions. She stopped minimizing her pain. She realized that tides weren't meant to drown her they were meant to teach her rhythm.

Tides

Life moved in tides rising and falling, giving and taking, pulling her forward and then back again. Amelia began to notice the pattern once she stopped resisting it. Every emotion, every season, every loss and return had its own timing. Nothing stayed high forever. Nothing stayed low forever. The tide always turned.

She learned to ride the waves instead of fighting them. Fighting had exhausted her left her gasping, angry at the water for doing what water does. So she softened. She listened. She let herself move with what was happening instead of bracing against it. In that surrender, something shifted.

She stopped apologizing for her emotions, recognizing they were not inconveniences but signals—messages from within asking to be honored. She stopped minimizing her pain, no longer shrinking her truth to make others comfortable. Her feelings were not too much; they were honest.

The tides taught her rhythm. They showed her when to advance and when to rest, when to speak and when to be still. Amelia realized the waves were never trying to drown her they were teaching her how to move with life, how to trust her own timing, how to stay standing even as the water rose around her.

Still Waters Speak Stillness frightened Amelia—because silence used to mean danger. But now she found comfort in quiet moments. In still waters, she began to hear her intuition speak clearly: You deserve more. You deserve softness. You deserve love that doesn't make you shrink. She didn't know that Terrance would be the first man to echo those truths back to her.

•••

Healing was never a straight line, no matter how much Amelia wished it could be. Some days arrived heavy, pulling at her ankles with doubt, disappointment, and the lingering ghosts of her childhood memories that surfaced without warning, like debris rising from the ocean floor. On those days, she felt the familiar ache in her chest, the old question whispering again: *Why did it have to be this hard?*

But this time was different. She no longer panicked when the water rose. She no longer fought the current until exhaustion set in. Instead, she remembered what survival had already taught her how to float. Disappointment still came in waves, crashing unexpectedly, but it no longer swallowed her whole. She learned to let the water carry her until the surge softened, until her breath returned.

Each wave left something behind clarity, strength, wisdom. Every rise and fall reminded her that resilience wasn't about avoiding pain; it was about trusting herself to endure it. And as the water settled again, Amelia realized she wasn't regressing—she was learning how to stay afloat in deeper waters, stronger and more certain than she had ever been before.

Love Letters to Myself

She began writing love letters not to a man, not to a future version of herself she was still chasing, but to the woman she already was. The one who survived. The one who stayed. The one who kept going even when no one was watching. Each letter became a quiet conversation, a place where she could tell the truth without fear of rejection.

She wrote things she had waited her whole life to hear:
I am worthy.
I am growing.
I am not my past.
The words didn't come easily at first. Some days her hand trembled, unsure if she believed what she was writing. But she wrote

anyway. Each sentence felt like a drop of water smoothing the sharp edges inside her—softening old wounds, easing the tight grip of self-doubt. Page by page, she began to see herself differently.

Healing wasn't perfect. Some letters were messy, tear-stained, unfinished. But they were honest. And in that honesty, Amelia discovered something powerful: the love she had been searching for had been waiting for her voice all along.

Amelia always loved writing. Long before she understood why words mattered, they had already chosen her. English was her favorite subject the only place where she consistently felt seen and it showed. Straight A's came easily when she could read between the lines, shape meaning, and give emotion a voice. She was rarely without a journal, carrying it like a lifeline, pages filled with thoughts she couldn't say out loud. Writing became her escape, her safe place, something almost magical a door she could open when the world felt too heavy. On the page, she wasn't powerless; she was the author. Every sentence was a release, every paragraph a breath. Over time, her pain learned how to move differently it softened, transformed, became poetry. What once hurt her began to heal her, and through writing, Amelia discovered that her voice could turn survival into something beautiful.

Flow became Amelia's new mantra not something she repeated aloud, but something she practiced in the way she breathed, moved, and finally let go. For most of her life, she had survived by pushing, forcing, bracing herself against whatever came next. But flow asked something different of her. It asked her to trust. Instead of forcing outcomes, she allowed moments to arrive as they were. Instead of chasing love, validation, or certainty, she opened her hands and received what was meant for her. And instead of drowning beneath expectations her own and everyone else's she learned how to float, discovering that possibility carried her more gently than fear ever had.

She began to slow down, honoring the small rituals that grounded her. Journaling became her river each page a release, each word a step closer to clarity. Meditation taught her how to sit with herself without judgment, to let thoughts pass like waves rather than pulling her under. She started noticing joy in places she once rushed past: sunlight spilling across the floor in the morning, the hush of early hours before the world demanded anything from her, the sharp, clean taste of cold water after a long day of holding herself together.

Flow was freedom not the loud kind, but the steady kind. The kind that doesn't need permission. The kind that arrives when you stop resisting who you are becoming. For the first time in her life, Amelia felt aligned with her own rhythm, moving at a pace that belonged to her. She was no longer fighting the current of her past or racing toward a future she couldn't control. She was here. Present. Breathing. And in that presence, she discovered that healing wasn't about fixing herself it was about allowing herself to be.

Amelia always loved writing. Long before she understood why words mattered, they had already chosen her. English was her favorite subject the only place where she consistently felt seen and it showed. Straight A's came easily when she could read between the lines, shape meaning, and give emotion a voice. She was rarely without a journal, carrying it like a lifeline, pages filled with thoughts she couldn't say out loud. Writing became her escape, her safe place, something almost magical a door she could open when the world felt too heavy. On the page, she wasn't powerless; she was the author. Every sentence was a release, every paragraph a breath. Over time, her pain learned how to move differently it softened, transformed, became poetry. What once hurt her began to heal her, and through writing, Amelia discovered that her voice could turn survival into something beautiful.

Amelia thought to herself "If I hadn't had my grandmother, I might have grown up believing that all women were cruel, distant, and unsafe just like my mother was to me". Amelia's grandmother was the balance. She was the proof. She showed Amelia what love looked like in action, how to grow into a young lady, how to appreciate who she was and recognize her worth. She spoke life into Amelia before she ever knew how much she would need it, always telling Amelia she was going to be something, even when her world suggested otherwise. And somehow, life kept placing incredible women in Amelia's path right when she needed them most. One of them was the principal of Amelia's high school the continuation school Amelia finally settled into in Los Angeles, where she was able to bring her babies with her and continue her education because they had on-site childcare. Her name was Miss C, an older Black woman with wisdom in her eyes and certainty in her voice. She told Amelia not *if* I graduated, but *when* and promised that when Amelia did, she would furnish her first apartment. Amelia didn't believe her at the time, but this was the same woman who helped Amelia get her first job, who believed in Amelia without making her beg, scrape, or borrow dignity. She saw Amelia. So did her math teacher, Miss T another brilliant, beautiful Black woman in education who never treated her struggle as a flaw. Later, when Amelia left Tyler and found herself in a shelter, it was yet another powerful Black woman Pat at WLCAC who helped Amelia secure housing, learn how to save my money, and grow in her career. Because of these women, and the many who came after them Amelia learned how to maintain a job, pursue education, and believe in herself without fear. They supported Amelia without jealousy, without doubt, without trying to dim her light. They wanted Amelia to be greater. So this is Amelia's shout-out to all the amazing Black women who truly care about another woman's success who see potential and nurture it. Amelia's life's goal has always been to carry that same spirit forward, to be that resource, that encouragement, that safe place so every Black girl, Black boy, and every human being, period, knows what it feels like to be cared for, supported, and loved.

Tears on My Pillow

My pillow knows the stories
I never learned to say out loud
the ones that fall from my eyes
when the world finally gets quiet
and the strong woman in me
lets her armor slip to the floor.

It holds the tears I hide from daylight,
the ones that burn, then cool,
like grief learning how to breathe.
Every drop a memory,
every memory a prayer,
every prayer a piece of me returning home.

Tears on my pillow
aren't weakness
they're release.
They're the truth my voice can't carry,
the healing my body whispers
when my mind tries to forget.

Tonight, they fall softly,
rhythmic and honest,
a language only my soul understands.
I let them come
let them speak
let them wash the ache from my chest
until my breath finally loosens.

And when morning comes,
my pillow may still be wet
but my heart...
my heart will be lighter
proof that even in the dark,
I am learning to save myself
one tear at a time.

Religion

Amelia raised in a household filled with religion but not truth.
The kind of religion that demanded obedience, silence, and performance, while excusing harm behind closed doors. Her mother and father preached holiness but practiced abuse. They were users, hypocrites, and violent in ways that never matched the words they shouted on Sunday mornings. Yet they wanted Amelia wanted us to believe *their* religion without question.
Church wasn't optional.
Church was constant.
Every day.
Twice on Sunday.
Shut-ins. Revivals.
Religion was not introduced as love.
It was enforced as control.
What they never preached about was hunger.
We were hungry.
Hungry on the streets.
Hungry with no money.
Hungry with empty cabinets and empty promises.

My mother gave **everything** to the church.
Her money.
Her welfare checks.
Her food stamps.
Even our clothes.
The church *knew* she had all these children. They saw them. They knew they were struggling. They knew they were hungry. And they did not care.

Because it was always said, *"In the name of God, He will bless you."*
That statement always felt idiotic to Amelia even as a child.
Amelia would think, *He already blessed you. You have money. You have food. Why are you giving it away?*
Amelia asked her mother once, "Mom, you have money. Why are you giving it away?"
Amelia got scolded.
"Don't go against God."
"This is God's will."
So God's will was for us to starve?
God's will was for us to be destitute?
God's will was for us to be homeless?
That question got me in trouble every time.
Amelia's mouth.
Amelia's refusal to stay quiet.
Amelia's inability to watch my family suffer and pretend it was holy.
Amelia and her siblings ate Top Ramen noodles **29 days out of the month.** Twenty-nine.
The one day she received her welfare check, they got a good meal. A burger from the burger stand. That day felt like luxury. Like relief. Like normal.
And then every dollar after that went straight to the church.
Amelia remembers one of her birthdays.
Patricia gave Amelia money to buy new clothes. Amelia could tell it wasn't easy for her. Amelia went to the store. She picked out clothes, tried them on.Sstood there, looking in the mirror, feeling normal feeling seen.
Then Patricia told Amelia she had to return all of it.
Every piece.
Because she needed the money to give to the church.
That moment broke more than Amelia's heart.

It cracked her faith.

Not just in men preachers but women preachers too. Women who had children of their own. Women who knew what it meant to feed a family. Women who stood in pulpits preaching sacrifice while watching children starve.

Amelia watched my mother take food out of **our refrigerator,** bag it up, and give it to her pastor.

Bag it up.

Hand it over.

While her own children went without.

That was religion.

One revival still lives in my body like a scar.

Patricia made sure all of her children always went up to the altar to be prayed for. Every time. But one day, Amelia and her siblings made a quiet agreement: *they would not fake it.*

Amelia stood in line.

Hands up.

Eyes closed.

The pastor poured what he called "holy oil" on Amelia forehead olive oil dressed up as divinity. He prayed in tongues the same tongues, the same sounds, every service. Then he asked, "Do you feel the Spirit?"

But he was pushing Amelia. Tilting her body. Trying to force her fall.

And Amelia told the truth:

"I feel you pushing me.

No, I don't feel anything."

That night, Amelia got the worst beating of her life.

From that moment on, Amelia was labeled *the devil.*

You don't question the preacher.

You don't question scripture even when it's being altered.

You don't question suffering even when it's unnecessary.

Religion did not protect Amelia.

Religion punished her.

So no I do not believe in religion Amelia stated.

"Religion is man-made.

But I **do** believe in the Most High God.

I believe He protected me when religion didn't.

I believe He walked with me through hunger, abuse, homelessness, and silence.

I believe it was never His intention for men to profit while children starved.
And still, the question follows me":

What is your religion?
(Amelia's inner thoughts)

I struggle with that today.
I don't argue with religious people anymore. I've learned that debates don't heal wounds like mine. But I do ask questions.
If there is only one God,
why are there so many denominations?
So many religions?
So many practices?
Why the Pope?
The priests?
The pastors?
The bishops?
Why so many gatekeepers to something that is supposed to be divine and accessible?
Religion, by definition, is a system—beliefs, rituals, and rules created by people. And people are capable of both good and great harm.
Faith is different.
Faith is personal.
Faith is quiet.
Faith doesn't need fear, force, or starvation.
My faith lives outside of buildings that once hurt me.
Outside of pulpits that demanded silence.
Outside of systems that broke children in the name of God.
I don't belong to a denomination.
I don't subscribe to fear-based worship.
I don't bow to men—or women—who demand obedience without accountability.
What I believe in now is relationship, not religion.
Truth, not performance.
A God who listens—even when I question.

And maybe that is my answer.
Not religion.
But faith that survived religion.
put in paragraph form

(Amelia thinking out loud)

At the age of fifteen, I met a guy named Christopher; he made me feel special. We dated for a while. One evening he invited me over to his place; we made what I imagined was love. After that, I really didn't want to see him anymore, so I avoided him. One evening, I was chatting on the phone with my best friend Shelby, and I felt something weird in my stomach, so I dropped the phone and rushed to the bathroom. I couldn't go, so I continued my conversation. Weeks passed. Months passed. I didn't receive my cycle. At this point, I became afraid. There was no way that I could tell my mother or anyone else. I missed school, too overwhelmed to focus on anything, and took myself to the free clinic near my house, praying the entire walk there that everything would be okay.

I checked in quietly, trying not to draw attention to myself. Sitting in that cold waiting room felt like the longest hour of my life. When the nurse finally called my name, my heart dropped to my stomach. She handed me a cup, and after what felt like forever, she returned with the results. "It's positive," she said softly. My whole world stopped. I felt like my body didn't belong to me anymore. I felt like a child trapped inside a nightmare that I couldn't wake up from.

I left the clinic in a daze, walking home with tears burning the back of my eyes but refusing to fall. I didn't know what to do. I didn't know who to turn to. I didn't want to be a mother. I didn't even know how to love or take care of myself. All I knew for sure was that there was no way I could bring an innocent child into the same broken home that had destroyed me.

So I tried to end the pregnancy on my own. I didn't have anyone to talk to. I didn't have support. I was terrified. But before I could do anything, my mother found out. And when she did, all hell broke loose. She screamed at me for trying to "embarrass" her, accused me of being fast, of being stupid, of being everything she always told me I would become. She didn't ask if I was scared or hurt. She didn't ask how I felt. She didn't even ask who the father was. Instead, she demanded that I keep the baby, telling me she wasn't paying for anything and that this was my "punishment" for being "grown."

Her words crushed me. I remember standing there, shaking, holding the wall so I wouldn't fall, thinking, *I'm only fifteen. I'm still a child. Why is my life already over before it even started?* But in my mother's house, I didn't have a say. I didn't have a voice. I didn't have a choice. And that was the moment I realized — whether I was ready or not — my childhood was officially gone.

A week later, I finally gathered the nerve to contact Christopher and tell him the news, not knowing how he would take it. I had been avoiding him, and now I had to call and inform him that I was pregnant. I prepared myself for the worst. The phone rang, and he answered, "Hello? Hello?" I finally responded, "Hello Chris, this is Amelia. How've you been?" No response. "Well, I know we haven't spoken in a while, but I do understand if, after you hear what I have to say, you'll have some reservations. Please… just hear me out." I took a deep breath. "Here we go. I went to the doctor to take a pregnancy test, and it was positive. And the only person I've been with is you." There was silence on the other end. "Hello, Christopher?" I said softly. He finally replied, "I'm here… whatever you decide to do, I'll be there for you. Are you okay? Do you need anything?" "No, I'm fine," I told him. "Thank you. I'll talk with you later." What a relief. For the first time in a long time, I felt like someone was willing to stand beside me.

In the winter of 2000, I went into labor. I contacted Christopher; he picked me up and took me to the hospital. I was in labor for ten hours. That night, Aspen and Ashlyn were born — both six pounds, ten fingers, ten toes, and most importantly, healthy. For a moment, I felt like life might finally be turning around.

Things seemed better after I had the children, but only because they added extra income to my mother's wallet. When my mother had money, she was happy — even if it was just twenty dollars in her pocket. The night before her benefits came, I told her the twins needed new clothing; they were getting bigger and would be three months old the next day. She exploded into one of her usual rants. "I have other children to take care of! Nobody told you to go out there and spread your legs, stupid bitch!" I walked away, went to my room, laid on my pillow, and cried all night long.

The next morning, I woke up to yelling — typical behavior in my house, but this time something felt different. My bedroom door flew open. "Bitch, get your shit and get the hell out of my house! You think you're gonna sit around and use me for my money? Bitch, you crazy in your head! You don't contribute to nothing here!" My mother stormed into the room and got in my face, screaming, "Get out! Get out! Take your bastard kids and get the hell out, bitch!" I walked over to my children, placed them in their stroller, and tried to stay calm.

Then there was a knock at the door. It was the police. My mother opened it and instantly started crying uncontrollably. "She hit me with a crowbar!" she lied. "All I do is try to love my children, but I can't do it anymore. I want her out. There's nothing else I can do for her." The police turned to me and said I had to leave or go to jail. "You're considered an adult because you have children," the officer said. I was blindsided. I wasn't allowed to retrieve any of my belongings — not mine, not my children's. Nothing.

I walked the streets for several hours before getting the courage to explain what happened to my children's father and ask for help. He understood and picked us up. He allowed me and the babies to stay with him.

As the years went on, I distanced myself from my mother, and eventually from my entire family and certain friends who were headed down the wrong path. I decided to live for myself and my children. At sixteen, I moved in with my children's father and his family. I checked myself back into high school, found a job, and raised two children. I was determined to make it — even though it felt like I was going from one bad situation to another. I poured out my heart to Christopher, their father, and at first he was very sympathetic.

•••

From day one, Christopher was there for me, supporting me and his children with no questions asked. I had been living at Christopher's parents' house for approximately six months, and at that point, I suggested we find a place of our own. He agreed at first. A week or two passed, and when I brought up the proposal again, everything changed. He snapped, "I don't have any bills! What makes you think I want to start paying bills now? And who knows if they're even my kids anyway?" I stared at him in disbelief. Our children were eleven months old, and now he suddenly didn't believe they were his? Then he added, "I think you should just find a place of your own. I'm not ready to be tied down to one woman. I'm still a young man." At that point, I just walked away and let him rant and rave by himself.

With the money I saved from working and babysitting, I started searching for an apartment. I had no luck finding a place on my own. I mentioned my situation to a classmate at school who happened to be looking for a roommate. I scheduled an appointment to view the apartment with her. The apartment was located in Baldwin Park, a small area outside of Los Angeles, in a fairly decent neighborhood. Everything worked out— the apartment was big enough for both of us and our children. We were able to get a great deal on the place because her aunt was the apartment manager, and she put in a good word for us even though she had only met me twice. Over the next month, things were fine. We split everything 50/50, and the apartment stayed clean.

But eventually, things took a turn. My roommate started leaving her children without informing me. Her life began spiraling out of control. She started drinking heavily and bringing home different men every night. It became unsafe and unpredictable. I felt like the environment wasn't good for my kids or for me. I ended up having to work things out temporarily with my children's father because I had nowhere else to go. But going back felt like moving backward. Living with him was like being in hell.

Living with Christopher again was supposed to be temporary, but it immediately felt like I had stepped back into a life I had been trying to escape. Things got worse almost as soon as I moved back in. He became distant, irritable, and cold, like the weight of responsibility suddenly became too heavy for him to carry. He went from being supportive and caring to barely speaking to me unless he wanted something. He stayed out late, coming home drunk, or not coming home at all. Sometimes he acted like the kids were a burden, and other times he pretended they didn't exist. The tension in the house grew so thick that even the babies could sense it—they cried more, slept less, clung to me constantly. I felt alone, even with him right there.

The nights were the worst. I would lie awake, staring at the ceiling, listening for the sound of him stumbling through the front door. I never knew what version of Christopher would walk in: the angry one, the careless one, or the silent one who didn't even acknowledge us. Every time he raised his voice or slammed a door, my heart raced. I kept telling myself it was temporary, that things would get better, but deep down I knew I had walked into a situation that was slowly breaking me.

The moment I knew I had to leave for good came unexpectedly. One night, we got into a heated argument over something small—

something pointless, something that didn't matter—but the rage in his eyes scared me. He yelled that he didn't ask for this life, didn't ask for kids, didn't ask to be tied down. As he talked, I realized he wasn't arguing with me—he was arguing with the responsibility of being a man, a father, a partner. And in that moment, I looked at my children sleeping on the bed beside me and thought, *I refuse to let them grow up feeling unwanted, the way I did.*

I knew I had to break the cycle.

The next morning, something in me snapped awake. I didn't cry. I didn't argue. I didn't explain. I just made a decision. I packed whatever I could carry while he slept and walked out of that house with my children in my arms. I didn't know where I was going, but anywhere felt safer than staying. It was the first time in my life I chose myself. The first time I chose peace over chaos, even if peace meant uncertainty.

Finding independence wasn't pretty or easy. I struggled. I hustled. I worked any job I could find—babysitting, fast food, cleaning houses. I went days without sleep, juggling motherhood, survival, and school. But every sacrifice was worth it because it brought me closer to the life I wanted for my children. I taught myself how to budget, how to save, how to advocate for myself. I learned to depend on no one but me. I learned to trust my instincts, trust my hustle, trust my strength. And slowly, brick by brick, I built a life that didn't revolve around fear.

The next turning point in my life came when I looked in the mirror one day and didn't recognize the girl I used to be—the scared child, the teenage mother, the abused daughter. For the first time, I saw a woman. A survivor. Someone who had walked through hell and kept moving. That reflection sparked something inside me: a desire to do more, to be more, to rise above everything that tried to break me. It was the moment I realized that my past didn't define me—it was shaping me into who I was meant to become.

From that point on, I stopped living in survival mode and started living with purpose. I began setting goals. I started dreaming again. I enrolled in programs, learned new skills, and connected with people who believed in me. My life wasn't perfect, but it was mine. And for the first time, I felt a sense of hope—real hope—that maybe, just maybe, I was destined for something greater than the pain I had grown up in.

Christopher's life took a turn for the worst after one night that would haunt him forever. He and one of his closest friends, Marcus, had been at their usual poker game at the local casino. Marcus was having the night of his life hitting big hand after hand, winning thousands. The energy was high, the crowd loud, the chips piling up in front of him like a small mountain. But not everyone at that table was laughing.

Two men who had been losing badly kept staring at Marcus and Christopher with hard eyes, throwing around threats disguised as jokes. "I don't give a damn how this end," one of them muttered, slamming his cards down. "One of y'all is gonna pay me back. I'm getting my money back, believe that." Christopher and Marcus brushed it off at first. They'd been playing poker for years and had heard plenty of drunken talk. It was supposed to be a professional game serious money, but still "friendly."

When they finally left the casino, Marcus stuffed the thick envelope of cash into his jacket. He looked proud, excited, a little overwhelmed. They walked out laughing, talking about what they were going to eat when they got home just two young men in their twenties trying to make life fun.

They split up and headed toward their cars. Before pulling off, Marcus called out, "I'm gonna stop by the liquor store real quick." Christopher paused. Something in his spirit tugged at him. "Bro, don't do that," he said. "You got too much money on you. Just go straight home." Marcus shrugged him off, smiling. "Man, I'll be in and out. I'm good."

He wasn't.

Christopher pulled out of the parking lot, but something felt wrong. His chest felt tight. His hands kept gripping the steering wheel like he was fighting off a bad feeling. Halfway down the block, he made a U-turn. "Let me just make sure he's straight," he thought. That decision would replay in his mind for years the moment he couldn't save his friend but was forced to witness the end.

When Christopher pulled into the liquor store lot, his heart dropped. Marcus was just stepping out of his car, counting his money, looking proud. Before he could call his name, another car screeched to a stop beside them. Christopher recognized the faces instantly — the men from the poker table. His stomach sank.

Time slowed.

The doors flew open.

Words were shouted.

A shotgun appeared shiny, black, cold.

Before Marcus could react, before Christopher could scream, before anyone could breathe, the blast echoed through the parking lot like a bomb. Marcus fell instantly, collapsing to the ground as the envelope of money scattered in the air and drifted like confetti in slow motion.

The men grabbed the cash off the ground what little they could scoop during their frantic escape then jumped back in their car and sped off. They didn't even look back. They didn't care who saw. They didn't care who they killed.

Christopher froze. For a moment, he couldn't move, couldn't breathe. His ears rang. His vision blurred. His best friend   his brother, the guy he grew up with lay there dying in front of him. Marcus's eyes were open but empty, his body still, his life gone in seconds. Christopher dropped to his knees, shaking, screaming for help that came too late.

And something inside him broke.

From that night forward, Christopher was never the same. The light he used to carry in his eyes disappeared. He became quieter, colder, angrier. He blamed himself for not stopping Marcus, for not dragging him home, for not turning around sooner. He replayed that shotgun blast in his mind every night, hearing it in his sleep. The guilt ate at him. The trauma closed him off. The pain hardened him.

The Christopher you once knew died that night with Marcus.

And the man who remained was living in a darkness he never found a way out of.

After Marcus was killed, the whole atmosphere in Christopher's parents' house changed. It felt like a shadow settled over everything over him, over us, over the walls, over the children. The Christopher I first fell for was gone. The man who used to smile, joke, hold our babies, and plan for our future turned into someone I barely recognized. His trauma swallowed him whole, and he didn't know how to fight his way out of it.

He turned to alcohol fast.

At first, it was a drink here and there to "calm his nerves." Then it became every night. Then all day. Then all the time. He started drinking as soon as he woke up. He never admitted it, but I could see it he was trying to drown the memory of Marcus's blood, that shotgun blast, and all the guilt he carried. Instead of talking, he drank. Instead of grieving, he drank. Instead of being present with us, he drank.

Our home became unstable, unpredictable, and tense. He would come home stumbling, slurring his words, smelling like alcohol from across the room. Sometimes he cried for hours, apologizing for things I didn't understand. Other times he was angry, breaking things, yelling at nothing and everything, fighting demons no one else could see. I tried to be patient. I tried to hold us together. I tried to understand. But you can't save someone who doesn't want to be saved, someone who is drowning in a bottle they keep refilling themselves.

The nights were the worst. I would hear him pacing the floor, talking to himself, replaying that night over and over. He barely slept. When he did sleep, he woke up sweating, shaking, screaming Marcus's name. The sound woke the babies. It woke everyone. Peace didn't exist anymore.

The more he drank, the more aggressive he became. Not always physically but emotionally, verbally, mentally. The pressure in the house felt like walking on broken glass every day. I never knew which version of him I would get the silent one, the sad one, the angry one, or the drunk one. The Christopher who used to protect me now scared me without even trying.

And the worst part? He didn't realize the damage he was causing. He didn't see how his pain was spilling over and drowning all of us. Trauma is contagious and, in that house, everybody caught it

I tried talking to him. He pushed me away.

I tried praying for him. He kept drinking.

I tried ignoring it. But the babies cried every night.

I tried staying strong. But I was breaking too.

It got to a point where every time he opened a bottle, I felt my chest tighten, wondering what version of hell that night would bring. I didn't feel safe. I didn't feel stable. I didn't feel seen. I felt trapped trapped in a house full of ghosts and grief, trapped with a man drowning in a storm he refused to face, trapped in a life that felt like a repeat of everything I had run from.

Christopher tried to stop me from leaving. The moment he realized I was taking the kids, everything inside him snapped. He rushed toward me, grabbed my arm, and pushed me so hard I fell to the floor. Before I could catch my breath, he slapped me across the face. The sting lit up my entire body, and instantly I had a flashback my mother towering over me, the fear, the helplessness, the pain I had promised myself I would never experience again. Something inside me cracked wide open.

I wasn't that little girl anymore.
I wasn't the silent child who had to endure abuse.
Not this time. Not in front of my children.

My hands shaking, my heart pounding, I scrambled toward the

kitchen and grabbed a knife. I didn't even think survival took over. I held it out in front of me, tears streaming down my face, and screamed, "If you touch me again, I swear I will protect myself!" I wasn't threatening him. I was defending the only thing I had left myself and my babies.

The moment he saw the knife, Christopher's eyes widened. But instead of calming down, he panicked. He bolted out of the house and ran out of my sight. A few minutes later, he called the police. When the officers arrived, I was standing there still shaking, the knife long gone from my hand, the babies crying behind me. I explained every detail of what happened the pushing, the slap, the fear, the flashback, the panic. One officer nodded slowly, taking it all in. The other walked over to Christopher.

They asked him if he wanted to press charges.

Still drunk, still angry, still lost in his hurt, he screamed "YES!" like he wanted power over me one last time. But the officers stayed calm. They told him, "If we take her, we have to take you, too." He froze. The truth slapped him harder than he had slapped me. He realized that pressing charges meant exposing everything he had done. It meant losing control. It meant consequences.

So, he dropped it.

I stood there holding my babies, exhausted, crying silently, waiting for someone to tell me what would happen next. The officers looked at me with more understanding than I had expected. One of them said, "Ma'am... you're free to go." And those words felt like oxygen.

I walked out of that house with my children no bags, no belongings, no plan, just survival and God's mercy. But I left. I lived. I made it out.

And I lived to see another day.

My first night out on my own didn't feel like freedom. It felt like fear wrapped in exhaustion. I had nowhere to go, no money for a hotel, and nowhere safe enough to rest. I pushed the stroller down the street, the twins bundled in blankets, the night colder than I expected. Their tiny breaths puffed against the air, and every sound a car door slamming, footsteps behind us, the rumble of engines made my heart jump. I kept looking over my shoulder, terrified Christopher would follow me, terrified the police would return, terrified of everything.

I ended up sitting on a bus bench with my children in my arms, rocking them while I tried not to cry. I kept whispering, "It's okay... Mommy's here," even though I didn't feel okay at all. My feet hurt. My face stung where he had slapped me. My hands were trembling from holding that knife. My chest felt tight, like I was carrying the weight of every bad thing that had ever happened to me. But I stayed awake the whole night, afraid to close my eyes, afraid something would happen if I let my guard down.

When morning finally came, I felt like I had survived a war.

That next day, I swallowed my pride and did something I had never done before: I asked for help. Asking wasn't easy it felt like giving up, like failing, like admitting I couldn't do everything alone. But surviving meant letting go of pride. I called the only person I trusted enough a friend from school who had always been kind to me. I told her everything. She didn't judge me. She didn't ask why I stayed so long. She just came to get me and the twins without hesitation.

She let me stay with her for a few days, and even though it wasn't perfect, it was safe. For the first time in months, I slept without fear of yelling, without the smell of alcohol, without walking on eggshells. I still woke up in the middle of the night, heart racing, hearing echoes of Christopher's voice or flashes of my childhood trauma. Healing didn't come overnight. Trauma doesn't leave just because you leave the house it lived in.

Starting over with nothing was the hardest part. I had two babies, no stable income, and barely any clothes. I lived out of bags, slept on couches, took buses to get to interviews, and worked whatever shifts I could find. I felt like I was constantly running from danger, from memories, from the version of myself that had been conditioned to suffer silently. I learned how to get formula from local programs, how to budget down to the last dollar, how to make one meal stretch into two or three.

Emotionally, I was broken in ways I didn't even understand yet. I didn't trust anyone. I didn't trust love. I didn't trust my own judgment. I kept expecting the world to hurt me, because that was all I had ever known. But every time I looked at my children sleeping beside me, I found the strength to get up and try again the next day.

Healing wasn't a straight line. Some days I felt strong and motivated, determined to build a new life. Other days, I felt overwhelmed, depressed, and scared of repeating cycles I desperately wanted to escape. But piece by piece, I started rebuilding not because anyone saved me, but because I chose to save myself. I learned that asking for help wasn't weakness; it was necessary. I learned that I didn't have to live in survival mode forever. And I learned that the most important thing I could ever give my children was a mother who refused to quit.

Little by little, I began to believe that maybe life had more to offer than pain. Maybe I could break generational curses. Maybe I could create a life filled with peace, stability, and love the kind of love I never received growing up.

The next chapter of my life didn't arrive all at once. It wasn't dramatic or loud. It came quietly, in small moments moments where I realized I wasn't the same scared girl who grew up in chaos, or the teenager running from pain, or the young mother carrying the world on her back. Slowly, I began stepping into someone new. Someone stronger. Someone wiser. Someone who had been shaped by fire but refused to burn.

After those first difficult weeks of couch-hopping and surviving day to day, I reminded myself that my children deserved more than instability. They deserved a mother who believed in the possibility of better, even when better felt far away. I found a small transitional housing program that accepted young mothers, and even though it wasn't glamorous shared bathrooms, strict rules, small rooms it was the first roof over our heads that didn't come with yelling, drinking, or violence.

That fresh start gave me room to breathe. I got the twins into daycare and started applying for jobs real jobs not just whatever paid cash under the table. I worked early mornings, late nights, weakens... whatever I had to do. I enrolled back in school, determined to finish my diploma. There were days I walked in exhausted, days I cried in the bathroom between classes, days I wanted to quit but I didn't. I couldn't. I had two little people watching me. Every victory, even the small ones, felt like a step toward a life I'd never seen but knew I deserved.

Emotionally, healing was slow painfully slow. Trauma showed up in ways I didn't expect. Loud voices triggered me. Arguments made me shut down. The smell of alcohol made me physically sick. I didn't trust anyone easily. I kept my circle small, my guard up, and my feelings buried deep. But every time I held my children, I reminded myself that breaking generational curses doesn't happen overnight. Healing starts with awareness — and I had more awareness than anyone had ever given me credit for.

The next chapter of my life was about learning how to love myself again or maybe for the first time. I started journaling. I started praying differently. I started talking to God the way I wished someone had talked to me when I was young gently, honestly, without judgment. I began unpacking the pain I had carried since childhood, the pain I had normalized for far too long. Some days the weight of it all felt like too much, but each time I released even a little, I felt lighter.

I learned that independence wasn't just about money or housing it was about emotional freedom. It was about refusing to let my past dictate my future. It was about reclaiming my identity after years of being silenced, shamed, and controlled.

And slowly, opportunities found me.

I started meeting women who understood my struggle, women who had overcome their own battles, women who believed in me even when I didn't fully believe in myself. I took parenting classes, life-skills workshops, and programs that taught me about confidence, boundaries, and self-worth the things no one taught me growing up.

The next chapter of my life was not perfect. I still stumbled. I still made mistakes. I still over gave, trusted the wrong people sometimes, and fought battles no one saw. But I also grew. I learned. I evolved. I discovered a fire inside me that had survived every storm. And I began to realize that maybe just maybe my story wasn't one of tragedy.

Maybe it was one of transformation.

The next chapter of my life was the beginning of who I was meant to become.

A few months into my new life, I received a call I never expected. It was Christopher. His voice sounded low, almost fragile. He apologized for everything — the drinking, the violence, the chaos, the fear. He told me he had checked himself into rehab. He was in counseling. He said he wanted to do better, be better, and asked if he could visit the twins. I hesitated, but I agreed. Not for him — for them. Every child deserves to know their father if it's safe. I truly believed people could change if they wanted to, and for the first time in a long time, it sounded like he wanted to.

He picked me up from work that day. At first, everything seemed normal. He asked how I'd been, how the kids were doing, how life was going. The conversation was calm, almost peaceful. For a moment, I thought maybe he really had changed. Maybe rehab had worked. But about ten minutes into the drive, everything shifted. As soon as we merged onto the 110 freeway toward the 101, the energy in the car changed.

Christopher's voice lowered.

Then sharpened.

Then cracked.

He asked me if I ever thought about getting our family back together. I breathed in slowly and told him the truth no. I explained gently that he was still early in recovery, still working through rehab, still healing. I told him I wished him well, but I couldn't go backward. His face tightened. His grip on the steering wheel changed. His breathing grew harder.

Then he snapped.

He slammed his foot on the gas so hard the car lurched forward. The speedometer climbed 70, 80, 90, over 100 miles per hour. Cars flew by us in blurs. He screamed, "TODAY WE ARE GOING TO DIE!" He turned and looked at me with a rage I had never seen before. "Did you hear me? I SAID WE'RE GOING TO DIE TODAY!"

I stared straight ahead, feeling strangely calm.

Trauma will do that to you.

You stop fearing the things meant to kill you.

He yelled, "YOU'RE CRAZY!"

I spoke quietly but firmly, "I'm not the one driving. I'm not threatening anyone's life. You are. You live and you die and if this is my time, I accept it."

My words seemed to sock him.

He jerked the steering wheel.

The car spun out of control.

Everything was sound and silence all at once   the screech of tires, the smell of burning rubber, the glass shattering, the metal twisting, the violent slam into the center divider. The airbags exploded. The world flipped. My body was thrown. I don't know how but I was ejected from the car, rolling across the pavement, then everything went black.

When I opened my eyes, I was lying in the middle of the freeway disoriented, dizzy, blood running down my nose and face. People gathered around me, yelling for help. Sirens echoed in my ears. Someone touched my shoulder and asked, "Are you okay? Can you hear me?" I tried to sit up, my head spinning, everything blurry. But all I could think about were my children. I didn't care about injuries. I didn't care about the paramedics. I didn't care about the chaos around me.

I needed to get to my babies.

I pushed myself up, wobbling but determined. The paramedics tried to stop me. "Ma'am, you need medical attention!" they insisted. I refused. "I have to get to my kids," I said. My voice shook, but my spirit didn't. I walked blood on my face, clothes torn, body aching down the off-ramp, step by step, until I made it to my destination. I picked up my children, held them tight, and thanked God that I was alive to do so.

Christopher survived, but everything between us died that day.

We never spoke again as partners. I never allowed us to be alone again. From then on, any visits he had with the twins went through his family. I stayed far away, safe, protected, and determined never to return to the chaos I fought so hard to escape.

Walking away from that car wreck — bruised, bloody, shaken but alive — was the beginning of the end of Christopher and Amelia's story.

And the beginning of my own rebirth.

You Live, You Die

Amelia awakened the way she had awakened too many mornings before slowly, painfully, and without her memories lined up in the right order.

Her eyelids felt heavy.

Her body felt foreign.

Her breath came shallow, tasting like iron and fear.

And then she saw it.

Blood.

Dried across her upper lip.

Crusted along her nose.

Trailing down her chin in a thin, cracked river.

Her nose was broken.

But pain wasn't what terrified her

the blank spaces in her memory were.

All she had was her last sentence

echoing through her skull like a warning she didn't understand:

"You live, you die."

She had whispered it.

She remembered that much.

Her voice had been shaking.

Her heart had been breaking.

Something inside her had already felt gone.
She sat up on the edge of the bed,
hands trembling as she tried to gather herself
from the pieces she had become.
Because this was the pattern she kept reliving:
unpredictable nights,
unseen bruises,
men who loved her violently
with jealousy, insecurity, control,
or the cold, deadly silence of narcissism.
Different faces.
Same storm.
She had survived jealous lovers who wanted to own her,
insecure men who treated her confidence like a threat,
controlling men who used love as a weapon,
narcissists who only loved the parts of her they could manipulate.
Every relationship had been a mirror
reflecting back the wounds she didn't want to face.
But last night…
last night was different.
Last night almost killed her.
She closed her eyes,
and like water rising after a storm,
flashes of memory came rushing back:
His hands gripping the steering wheel too tight.
His voice thick with anger, swelling with something unhinged.
The car jerking forward.
The red lights he didn't stop for.
The freeway lanes blurring into chaos.
And then the words she would never forget:
"We gonna die tonight."
Her breath hitched at the memory.
She remembered the way his eyes looked in that moment
dark, hollow, gone.
She remembered his foot slamming on the gas.
The car shooting onto the freeway.
Her screams swallowed by the engine's roar.
Then the headlights

coming at them from the wrong side of the road.
He was driving against the traffic.
Against survival.
Against reason.
Against life.
She remembered grabbing the door handle.
She remembered praying.
She remembered feeling the world tilt beneath her.
And then nothing.
Blackness.
Silence.
Until she woke up,
in the middle of a cold road,
on her hands and knees,
blood dripping onto the asphalt
like her body was writing its own eulogy.
Cars had stopped.
Lights flashed.
Voices shouted.
Someone touched her shoulder and asked if she could hear them.
She hadn't known where he was.
She hadn't known if he survived.
She hadn't known how she got out.
But she knew one thing:
She was still alive.
And the question rose inside her like a scream:
"Is this how my story ends?"
For a long moment, she looked at the night sky,
the streetlights blurring into halos,
the air thick with gasoline, dust, and fear.
And she realized something terrifying:
She had come closer to death
in the hands of someone who claimed to love her
than she ever had in the hands of a stranger.
The truth tasted bitter,
stinging her tongue,
shaking her spirit:

**If she went back,
she wasn't living
she was dying in pieces.**
She pressed her palm to her chest.
Her heart was still beating.
Fragile but beating.
Blood on her face.
Bruises on her arms.
But breath in her lungs.
And breath meant choice.
She wiped her mouth,
rose on shaking legs,
and whispered the new version of her old words:
>**"I live.
>I don't die.
>Not for love.
>Not for him.
>Not like this."**
That night didn't break her.
It baptized her.
It washed away denial.
It forced her to see the truth buried inside her wounds.
She wasn't meant to die on a freeway
next to a man who never cared if she survived.
She was meant to live.
To heal.
To tell her story.
To walk through the world with the kind of strength
that comes only from surviving what should have destroyed you.
And as the ambulance lights flashed over her face,
Amelia realized something she had forgotten long ago:
Some storms come to drown you.
But some storms come to teach you how to breathe underwater.
This was the night she stopped dying by degrees.
This was the night she chose herself.
This was the night she truly began to live.

Cosmic Remembrance
When My Soul First Knew Love

Before love ever touched my skin,
before pain ever carved its first lesson,
I was star matter
pure light wrapped in possibility.

I remember the place before here,
the space between breath and becoming,
where souls float like lanterns
in an endless night sky,
speaking in frequencies instead of words,
healing through harmony instead of hands.

In that realm,
my spirit learned its first religion:
Love as creation.
Love as law.
Love as the original language.

I was formed in a galaxy
where every star is a teacher,
every nebula a womb,
every comet a messenger
carrying truth across eternity.

I came into this world
already knowing the sound of God
not a voice,
but a vibration,
a rhythm humming in my bones
reminding me:
You were born from brilliance.
You were crafted from cosmos.
You are the sky remembering itself.

And when life grew heavy,
when trauma tried to eclipse my heart,
I felt the universe rearranging around me,
guiding me through storms
I didn't yet have the strength to name.

Because I am never alone.
I walk with a constellation of ancestors
warriors, healers, mothers, dreamers
their spirits orbiting mine
like moons refusing to abandon their planet.

They stitched courage into my spirit
long before I learned fear.
They placed ancient wisdom in my blood,
a survival code
that activates whenever I am close to breaking.

Their whispers rise like tides inside my chest:
Remember who you are.
Remember whose you are.
Remember the universe lives in you,
not around you.

When I close my eyes,
I can feel the hands of generations
lifting me by the spine,
aligning me back to purpose,
back to power,
back to the truth
that I am the continuation
of a story written in the heavens
long before I touched earth.

I am cosmic memory.
Ancestral fire.
Celestial resilience wrapped in human skin.

And every time I choose love
deep love,
true love,
self-love
I align myself with the universe
that dreamed me into existence.

This is my origin.
My inheritance.
My eternal return
to the divine within me.

•••

Amelia's life closed like a heavy door one she never wanted to open, yet one she carried everywhere inside her. Childhood had never been kind to her; it had been a tide that rose too fast, swept her under too young, and taught her early how to breathe underwater just to survive. The years she spent being uprooted, mistreated, beaten, and silenced had filled her body with memories she couldn't fully name but could always feel. They lived inside her the way water lives inside a riverbed, shaping it quietly, relentlessly, changing it forever. What she didn't speak stayed inside her muscles, her breath, her heartbeat. The trauma she endured wasn't gone; it had simply settled into her like deep water waiting to be understood. And now, at the close of this chapter of her story, that water finally began to speak.

She could feel the truth of her emotions rising in her the way the ocean pulls itself toward the moon. They came not as explosions but as gentle waves at first the ache in her chest when certain memories returned, the sting of tears she never let fall, the tightness in her throat when she thought about the little girl she used to be. She realized that water had always been with her: in the tears she swallowed, in the rain that beat against the windows of every house they fled from, in the showers where she cried quietly so no one could hear, in the ocean she stood before as a teenager, wondering if it saw her the way she felt endless, rising, never still.

She understood now that water wasn't weakness; it was evidence. A sign that she had survived long enough to feel anything at all. Water had held her secrets, softened her wounds, and taught her that emotions were not her enemy. They were her release. They were her truth. They were her humanity. She realized that water had always shown up in her life as different versions of herself sometimes a quiet stream guiding her toward reflection, sometimes a storm demanding that she face what she had buried, sometimes a well of stillness reminding her to breathe. She could name every form of that water now: river for direction, rain for cleansing, ocean for depth, tide for movement, storm for transformation, tear for truth. Water carried her memories and washed over her pain until it became something like wisdom. It whispered to the wounds of her childhood, promising they did not have to stay open forever.

But water didn't just soothe her it prepared her.

Because once the water softened what had hardened inside her, something else began to rise. Something hotter. Something sharper. Something she didn't yet know how to understand but could feel burning quietly beneath her ribs.

This was Fire.

It started as a spark, the kind that flickered when she began to question the lies, she had been raised in the belief that she was unlovable, unworthy, unwanted. The spark grew when she realized she did not have to inherit her mother's pain. It flared when she survived things that should have broken her. Fire pushed against everything that tried to silence her. It was the part of her that refused to stay small, the part that refused to drown. Even when life kept trying to put her out, something inside Amelia kept burning. This flame whispered to her that she was meant for more than survival. It urged her to rise, to move, to grow, to refuse the title of victim even when life tried to tattoo it on her skin. Fire told her that her past was not a prison it was proof. And at that moment, Amelia realized that water had taught her to feel, but fire would teach her to fight.

She did not know it fully then, but the fire inside her would become the very thing that saved her. It would push her out of the darkness she was raised in, guide her toward her identity, and remind her that she could choose a life different from the one she inherited. As the water within her settled into truth, the fire rose to sculpt her future, setting the stage for the next part of her journey. And with that, she stepped into the next element of her becoming Tale, the Fire where the story of her survival would transform into a story of her rising.

•••

Water had followed Amelia her entire life, long before she had the language to understand that it represented emotion. It lived inside her chest when fear tightened her breath, in the tears she swallowed for survival, and in the quiet storms she carried through childhood without ever speaking a word. As she grew older, she began to understand that water was not just something that happened to her it was something she was. The weight of emotion pressed against her ribs like a rising tide, reminding her that feeling too deeply had once felt like drowning, especially in a home where emotions were punished, and silence was the only safe language. Yet slowly, she learned that water only overwhelms you when you try to fight it; when you surrender, it teaches you how to float. Music became her lifeline during the worst storms the blue notes her grandmother played, the soft hum of late-night radio, the melodies drifting from passing cars. In sound, she found shelter. She realized that even sadness had rhythm and even storms carried songs. Music wrapped around her pain and made it something she could breathe through.

There came a day when she finally stood before a mirror long enough to see herself clearly not the frightened little girl she once was, not the bruised teenager who tried to disappear, but the woman healing beneath all the memory. She touched the glass gently, whispering an apology and a promise to herself: "I'm here now. I came back for you." From there she learned that mirrors didn't only reflect damage; they reflected possibility. Still, storms inside the body don't vanish on command. Sometimes memories returned like heavy rain, sudden and overwhelming. But instead of running from these internal downpours, she learned to sit with herself gently, to breathe through the emotional flooding, to treat herself with the patience she would offer a frightened child. And slowly, the rain inside her became something she could survive.

Amelia carried memories of friendships too brief, tender, complicated childhood bonds that couldn't survive the constant uprooting of her life. One friend in particular lived in her memory like a river that had once flowed beside her but eventually drifted into its own direction. She didn't hold anger toward that separation; she understood that sometimes life pulls people apart not out of malice, but out of necessity. The ocean became her sacred place, the one place she could release everything without apology. She whispered grief into waves, let the saltwater wash over her ankles, and prayed silently for all the versions of herself she had outgrown or abandoned. The tide always returned, reminding her that healing, like water, comes in cycles.

Bathwater held her secrets long before she had words for them; it was where she hid her tears as a child, letting water muffle what she wasn't allowed to express. Later, it became a place of truth and cleansing, a space where submerged memories rose gently to the surface. Cooking became another quiet ritual of release; she seasoned rice with tears she didn't bother to wipe away and realized that some meals tasted like grief, some like healing, and some like both. She began to understand that a large part of her emotional weight wasn't hers alone it was inherited. The women who came before her carried their own storms, passing down pain the way water passes down currents. She felt this generational heaviness in her bones but vowed that she would be the one to break the cycle, transforming inherited storms into rain that nourished instead of destroyed.

Healing brought her to the calm after the storm, a quiet stillness she had never known as a child. It wasn't the absence of pain but the acceptance of truth. Peace crept into her life gently, whispering that she no longer had to fight everything she felt. She learned the beauty of flow the art of moving with life rather than against it, the practice of surrendering without giving up. As a June-born Cancer, she finally embraced her watery nature: emotional, intuitive, deeply feeling, ruled by the moon. These traits, once mocked or dismissed, became her power. She began writing love letters to herself in journals —small, tender poems and apologies to the girl she used to be. Through these words, she stitched her heart back together.

Silence, which once felt terrifying, became her sanctuary. Still waters taught her that quiet is not weakness it is strength, it is observation, it is wisdom. Healing came in tides: sometimes she receded, sometimes she returned, but she always found her way back to herself. She learned to forgive herself by imagining every old version of her dissolving into a pool of water, breaking apart like sand and washing away. She honored her boundaries the way one honors a weather forecast, learning to say, "Not today," when her emotional capacity was low. Through dreams and intuition, she felt the presence of the women who came before her ancestors who guided her like waves pulling gently toward shore. And finally, she discovered soft power, the truth that real strength does not shout, does not force, does not harden. Real strength is soft enough to cry, brave enough to feel, and wise enough to heal. Through the water within her, Amelia learned to rise.

•••

Amelia stood in front of the mirror and placed her hand over her heart, feeling the steady thrum beneath her palm as if her body were reminding her, You're still here. She lifted her eyes slowly, not to criticize or judge, but to finally meet the woman who had carried her through every storm. "I see you," she whispered, and the reflection staring back at her softened. Looking deeper, she saw the little girl inside herself the one who had been silenced, forgotten, overlooked. "You went through things you should have never experienced," she breathed. "You survived more than people will ever know. I'm sorry no one protected you." Tears gathered in her eyes, but this time she didn't swallow them; she let them fall, letting the truth wash over her. She reached toward her reflection as if offering comfort to a version of herself who had waited years for this moment. "Thank you for not giving up. Thank you for showing up even when you were hurting. Thank you for carrying us through storms we didn't deserve." Her voice trembled, but she kept speaking, feeling each word settle into her spirit like truth finding a place to rest. "You deserve peace. You deserve rest. You deserve love that doesn't hurt. You deserve to take up space." She looked at her face every scar, every curve, every sign of survival and something inside her finally exhaled. "I forgive you for the times you hid," she whispered. "I forgive you for the mistakes you made while trying to survive. I forgive you for loving people who couldn't love you properly. I forgive you for abandoning yourself... you didn't know better." Her tears slowed, replaced by a quiet strength that felt like the beginning of a new chapter. She spoke her name with intention: "My name is Amelia... and I'm becoming whole. My name is Amelia, and I'm learning to love myself. My name is Amelia, and I am worthy of joy." Then she looked deeper, past her own eyes, into the stories her blood still carried, the tales she never told, the truths she'd buried beneath survival. "I got more stories to tell," she said aloud, her voice steady. "More Tale. More Tail. More truth than trauma." She felt her reflection rise with her, mirroring her breakthrough. "I promise to choose you," she whispered. "I promise to protect you. I promise to listen to you. I promise to love you the way you always needed." The room fell silent, almost sacred, as if the air itself held space for her transformation. Amelia wiped her face, offered her reflection a gentle, knowing smile, and whispered to herself, "I am no longer hiding. I'm coming home... and I've got more stories to tell."

When Love Is Absent, What Changes in You?

When love is absent,
something subtle shifts
quiet at first, like a room inhaling,
like the soul pulling its own shadow closer
just to feel held.

You start listening differently.
To the walls.
To the silence.
To the parts of you you once ignored
because someone else's voice was louder
than your own heartbeat.

When love is absent,
your body remembers.
It remembers the weight of loneliness,
the heaviness of nights spent
convincing yourself you're not the problem.
It remembers the cold.
The ache.
The empty space beside you
that used to feel like home.

Your smile changes
still there, but softer,
a little cracked at the edges
like stained glass
still trying to catch the sun.

Your spirit changes too.
You move differently
not broken,
but cautious,
like someone relearning how to walk
after trusting the wrong ground.

You start loving yourself in places
you once abandoned.
You water the wilted corners.
You patch the holes.
You dust off dreams
you buried beneath someone else's comfort.

Because when love is absent,
you learn to become your own presence.
Your own warmth.
Your own truth.
Your own survival.

You rise
not because someone loved you,
but because you finally remembered
you were never meant
to live without love...
especially the kind
that begins within.

Love Is Proven In The Storms

You ever notice...
how **anybody** can love you in the sunshine?
When your smile is loud,
your spirit is calm,
and the world feels soft enough to sleep on?

But babyyy
real love...
real love is born in the storm.
It's the thunder that makes your heart misstep.
The rain that exposes everything you tried to hide.
The lightning that flashes truth across the sky
so bright you can't pretend you don't see it.

Real love...
breathes through the chaos.
It lives in the shaking hands
that still reach for each other
when pride says, "Turn away."

It's the whisper
barely a whisper
"I'm not leaving,"
spoken through a throat tight with tears.

It's when patience is thin,
voices are sharp,
and both of y'all are tired
down to the bone
but you still stay.
You still try.
You still fight *for* each other,
not *with* each other.

Let me tell you something...
Love ain't proven in the pretty.
Mm-mm.
Anybody can show up when it's easy.

Love is proven
on the nights
you almost fall apart
but don't.

On the nights
when silence is louder
than every argument you've ever had,
and you're sitting on opposite sides of the bed
breathing confusion...
but you don't walk away from the room.

You breathe anyway.
You stay anyway.
You reach anyway.

That reach?
That right there?
That's love.

Love is holding somebody's pain
as if it's your own.

It's forgiving
when your pride is screaming,
"No. Not this time."

It's seeing their tears
and feeling them in your own throat.

It's ugly.
It's messy.
It's exhausting.
It's honest.

And somehow…
somehow it heals you too.

Because love isn't a fair-weather friend.
It doesn't disappear when the winds pick up.
It doesn't fold when the pressure rises.

Love stands in the center of the storm,
rain soaking its skin,
lightning on its tongue,
heart wide open
and it says:

**"Us.
I choose us."**

Not once.
Not twice.
But every time the clouds gather
and the sky goes dark.

Love is proven
in the chaos.
In the trembling.
In the breaking moments
that somehow knit you back together.

In the hands
that keep reaching
through every storm
again
and again
and again.

•••

It was a cool Friday night outside Hot & Cool Café, the kind of night that feels charged with possibility. The drum circle echoed from the plaza, scents of incense and roasted corn drifting through the air. People gathered in clusters artists, poets, community elders, teenagers with notebooks each person a story waiting to be heard.

Amelia sat on the curb, notebook open on her lap, pen tapping rhythmically as she wrote the truth she'd avoided for years:

"I wasn't raised with love.
But I am determined to learn it anyway."

She read it twice, feeling her heart press against her chest.

"You write like you hiding something," a voice said.

She looked up.

A man stood a few feet away **Jordan Rivers.**

Tall. Strong. Tattoos running down his forearms like prayers written in ink. His eyes held a quiet storm, something wounded but controlled. He had a sketchbook in his hand, and Amelia realized he'd been drawing her.

His gaze wasn't invasive it was knowing. Like he recognized pain the way a survivor recognizes another survivor.

She didn't know yet that Jordan would become the fire of her story the part that burns and transforms.

Before she could respond, another voice called her name from behind.

Zora Mayfield approached in her work uniform, her curly hair pulled into a messy bun, the energy around her sharp but warm. Zora had the presence of someone who ran into danger for a living and still kept her humor intact. She had come to support her cousin Shaq at the open mic, but the moment she saw Amelia, her eyes softened with curiosity as if sensing a connection neither of them could explain yet.

Zora would become the tail of the story
the unexpected twist,
the truth hidden in shadow,
the woman whose path would collide with Amelia's in life-changing ways.

"Some nights save you. This was one of mine."

Amelia always found her love in writing.

Words were her oxygen long before she knew she'd been suffocating. Writing was the only place where she could inhale without fear, without judgment, without someone's voice drowning her own. It was her refuge—a soft corner in a world made of sharp edges. Each notebook she filled became another room in a home she built out of paper because the one she lived in never felt like hers.

Whenever her mother put her out—clothes flying, insults thrown like stones—Amelia carried her backpack like a lifeline. She wandered the cracked sidewalks of Los Angeles with her heart sitting heavy in her chest and her notebooks tucked under her arm. The city became her shelter. The glow of streetlights became her candles. The rhythm of cars on Crenshaw soothed her the way a lullaby should have.

She found solace in the places where broken people went to feel alive.

Kings & Queens of Poetry + Music, Diverse Verses LA, Leimert Park. SWAMM Da Poetry Lounge. Hot & Cool Café.

Rooms lit only by dim bulbs and raw truth. Places where shadows leaned against walls and stories clung to the air like smoke. Any space with a microphone felt like a confessional booth for the wounded, and Amelia—quiet, observing—felt safest in the back of the room.

She hid beneath a hoodie, her curls tucked away, her voice

locked deep inside her ribcage. From that corner, she watched poets rip themselves open onstage, turning trauma into testimony. Pain into lyric. Shame into liberation. Their voices rose and fell like ocean tides, like earthquakes, like sermons. She admired the courage in their trembling hands, the fire in their throats, the way the audience embraced vulnerability as if it were holy.

She wanted to be that brave.

But bravery was a language she hadn't learned yet.

Writing was her secret world.

Speaking… was a battlefield.

One night—a night heavy with sorrow, after another fight that left her standing outside her mother's door with nowhere to go—Amelia followed her feet to a local open mic. Her heart felt like cracked glass. Her notebook felt heavier than usual, swollen with words that refused to stay quiet any longer.

Inside the venue, the air smelled of incense and warm bodies. The lights were low, the bassline of someone's poem vibrating through the floor like a heartbeat. Amelia approached the sign-up sheet, her hands trembling so violently she almost dropped her pen. Fear begged her to sit down, stay invisible, keep surviving in silence.

But something inside her stronger, older, ancestral whispered:

Tonight, you speak.

She wrote her name.

Her whole world shifted with that single signature.

Time slowed.

Minutes stretched out like long hallways.

Every performer before her felt like a countdown she wasn't ready for.

Then the host returned to the mic, scanned the list, and smiled.

"Next up… Amelia."

Amelia's name was called for the mic.

She stood up slowly, notebook pressed to her chest. Her palms were sweating not from fear, but from the weight of finally speaking the truth she'd carried for decades.

The crowd quieted as she stepped onto the small stage.

Jordan leaned against the wall, eyes fixed on her.

Zora crossed her arms, studying her like a puzzle piece she wasn't ready to place yet.

Amelia inhaled deeply and let her truth pour out:
In her mind she repeated her poem
"I wasn't raised with love.
But I deserve it.
And tonight...
I'm choosing myself."
The room stilled.
And in that moment
the universe shifted.
Her healing began.
And all three of their stories silently intertwined.

Her breath caught. Her heart stopped. Her legs moved anyway.

She walked toward the stage as if pulled by something greater than courage. The crowd became a blur of silhouettes. Heat from the spotlight wrapped around her like a question she was finally ready to answer. She took the microphone cold, heavy, trembling in her hand and when she opened her notebook, the room fell away. Everything outside the page went dark, muffled by the pounding of her pulse.

The fear she'd carried since childhood cracked open.

And she began to read.

Her voice quivered like a match struggling to stay lit, but she kept going line after line, memory after memory, wound after wound.

She spoke of abandonment, of growing up unseen, of walking through Los Angeles searching for love in a city that taught her violence first. She confessed every truth she had swallowed: the nights she cried into her journal, the days she wished someone would just hold her, the way writing saved her life when people tried to destroy it.

As the final words left her lips, something unlatched in her chest.

A loosening.

A release.

Like she had peeled off years of silence in one breath.

A sacred silence held the room for one heartbeat.

Then the audience exploded. People rose to their feet, clapping, cheering, snapping, stomping.

Voices crashed around her:
"YES!"
"Talk yo shit!"

"Another one!"
"Say that!"
They weren't applauding the poem.
They were applauding *her survival.*

For the first time in her life, Amelia felt seen truly, deeply seen. Not as the strong one, not as the quiet one, not as the girl who endured too much but as a woman with a voice powerful enough to silence a room.

She stepped off the stage, breathless, notebook pressed tight to her heart.

A warmth spread through her chest, a feeling she had never known before, something like pride and relief and belonging.

She whispered to herself:

"This is mine. This is for me. I found my voice."

And in that moment, she knew everything had changed. She would never return to silence again. Her voice her truth had finally risen from the shadows.

And she wasn't going back.

I Am the Flame That Never Asked for Permission to Burn

When Amelia Meets Fire: Zora Mayfield

Amelia met Fire long before she ever understood she was capable of burning. It happened on a night that felt ordinary at first the kind of warm Los Angeles night where the city's breath hangs soft in the air, steady, familiar, exhausted. She slipped into The Ember Lounge, an underground space disguised beneath an abandoned storefront, its walls painted matte black, its stage lights low and glowing like bruised sunsets. That was the night she first saw her. Zora Mayfield. A woman who didn't simply walk she ignited the ground beneath her. Tall, striking, with hair that moved like a flame finding its own rhythm, Zora carried a presence that wasn't loud but demanded attention all the same. She made people lean in before she ever opened her mouth. Amelia felt it immediately that heat, that warning, that quiet invitation to step closer even though something inside her whispered she wasn't ready.

Zora stepped onto the stage wearing red hoops and a confidence Amelia had never been allowed to taste. The mic didn't just fit in her hand it bowed to her, like even sound itself understood who it belonged to. And then she spoke. Her voice cracked open the ceiling and spilled truth across the room, vibrating through Amelia's ribs with a force she forgot she could feel. Zora didn't perform her poem she lived inside every syllable. She told a story about women who survived generational fire women who learned to cook from flames meant to consume them, women who danced barefoot across broken memories, women who turned smoke into prayer. Every line landed somewhere deep in Amelia, awakening something she thought she had drowned years ago. She realized she had been surviving water for so long she never imagined Fire could feel like home.

When the poem ended, there was no applause not because the audience didn't want to clap, but because they were too stunned to remember how. In the hush, Zora's eyes found Amelia's. She didn't smile or nod; she simply saw her saw straight through her as if she were a candle trying to hide its own flame. Amelia looked away first, not out of intimidation but because something inside her flickered for the first time in years. A tiny, trembling spark. What was that? she whispered to herself.

After the show, Amelia lingered in the hallway pretending to read a flyer. Zora walked past smelling like honey and smoke, and without even looking fully at her asked, "You write?" The question struck Amelia like a match head. She nodded. "Yes... but I haven't performed in a long time."

Zora tilted her head, watching her with a quiet certainty. "That's because your fire's sleeping," she said. "Not gone. Just waiting on you." Amelia's chest tightened. She tried to laugh it off, but Zora leaned in, her voice low and warm. "You got heat under all that water. I felt it from the stage." Amelia didn't know whether to run or stay, but heat rose in her body anyway. Nobody had ever spoken to her like that like she was powerful, not fragile. Like she was more than the storms she had survived.

"Teach me," Amelia said quietly. "Teach me how not to be afraid." Zora smirked, her eyes glowing like coals. "Oh, Amelia. You're already brave. You survived what should've killed you. I'm just here to show you how to use what's left."

From that night on, they became something neither of them had a name for not friends, not sisters, but something deeper, ancient, soul-recognizing. Zora taught Amelia breathwork, grounding, courage, stage presence, the difference between hiding and healing. She taught her how to let her voice break without apologizing for its cracks. And Amelia, without realizing it, taught Zora the art of stillness. The quiet grace of reflection. The intuitive gentleness Fire secretly craves in order not to burn itself out. Together, they were steam storm hot rain on summer pavement. Zora told Amelia her poetry felt like standing in the rain and remembering she had once been lightning. Amelia told Zora her words felt like surviving a house fire and discovering the heart didn't burn.

One night, Zora placed a mic in Amelia's hand. "You're up," she said. "No more hiding." Amelia's hands trembled as old ghosts rose the church shame, her mother's silence, the fear she had swallowed so many years it had its own pulse. But Zora stood behind her like a steady flame waiting to be caught. "Your fire doesn't have to be loud to be real," she whispered. Amelia exhaled. When she stepped onto the stage, it wasn't the flood that carried her it was the flame. Her voice wavered, cracked, and then caught fire. She spoke her truth: the little girl who grew up without hugs, the teenager who survived violence, the young woman who lost herself trying to be loved. But she didn't burn down she burned through. The audience fell silent. Zora wiped a single tear, fierce and proud.

After she stepped offstage, breathless and trembling, Zora pulled her close. "There she is," she said softly. "The woman who survived the flood and still found a way to burn." Amelia smiled, and for the first time in her life, she wasn't afraid of her fire. She wasn't afraid of herself.

She had finally met the flame that lived inside her.

The Fire Inside Amelia

Fire always lived inside Amelia long before she knew it had a name, long before she recognized it as hers. It began as a quiet spark curled deep in her belly when she was still small enough to swing her legs off the edge of a church pew. A small glow that flickered behind her ribs every time someone tried to silence her. She didn't yet know that the spark was survival disguised as heat that inside every quiet girl lives a flame waiting for the right breath, the right moment, the right hurt, to rise.

She grew up watching her mother hide her own fire under layers of exhaustion, secrets, and swallowed screams. Amelia learned early that some women burn quietly because the world teaches them loud flames get punished. But even as a child, even while life poured bucket after bucket of water on her spirit, Amelia felt a pull inside her a tremor, a warmth, a stubborn whisper that refused to die. That whisper sat behind her heartbeat like a warm ember under winter ash, glowing even when everything around her felt cold.

She would one day tell herself, "I am the flame that never asked for permission to burn."

But back then, the truth wasn't words it was sensation.

A throb in her chest when she watched her father punch holes into thin apartment walls.

A heat behind her eyes when her mother shrank at the sound of his footsteps.

A smolder in her throat every time she tried to speak and was told to "stay quiet," "stop crying," or "be strong like a big girl."

That last phrase confused her the most how could she be strong and silent at the same time?

Strength vibrated inside her bones like a caged animal; silence smothered it like a wet blanket. Fire wanted to roar, but fear kept forcing it down into embers.

She remembered nights when she and her twin sister lay side by side in the dark, both pretending to sleep while chaos cracked like thunder against the walls. Every scream from the next room struck her like a match. Every slammed door sent sparks flying beneath her skin. She wasn't afraid of the noise she was afraid of what the noise awakened in her.

Heat. Anger. The impossible desire to stand up and shield her mother even though she was too small to reach the doorknob. She didn't want the world to burn. She just wanted the truth to stop hiding. She wanted her mother's shadow to step back into its body. She wanted someone anyone to tell her that fire wasn't always dangerous. That fire could be courage. That fire could be enough. Outside, the wind would rattle the windows, sweeping through the cracks under the door like an invisible guardian. Amelia believed the wind was talking to her—urging her to stay awake, to stay aware, to someday use her voice the way fire uses heat: not only to destroy, but to illuminate. She didn't yet know that the wind and fire inside her were destined to meet, merge, and become her greatest truth:

When you stop asking for permission, you become unstoppable.

As she grew older, her fire changed shape. It learned manners. It learned restraint. It learned to fold itself into small, polite flames that flickered behind smiles and apologies she didn't owe. This was the era of candlelight a soft, obedient glow that offered warmth but refused to call attention to itself. She became good at pretending she wasn't burning.

"I'm okay." "It's fine." "Don't worry about me."

She wore these phrases the way some girls wore charm bracelets pretty distractions hiding deeper truths. Inside, though, her fire simmered like a pot left on low heat, waiting for someone to lift the lid. She felt that heat when teachers dismissed her intelligence. When boys mistook her confidence for arrogance. When family members called her "too emotional," "too sensitive," "too much." She never understood why her emotions scared people or why people thought they had the right to dictate the temperature of her soul. But fire doesn't forget. Fire keeps score.

And Amelia was keeping receipts.

By her teenage years, she could feel her fire in her body before she ever heard it in her voice. Heat collected behind her sternum whenever she swallowed her truth. Her palms tingled with words she wasn't allowed to say. Her jaw tightened each time someone tried to force her into shapes she didn't fit. She eventually learned the danger of bottling fire:

When fire has nowhere to go, it turns inward.
It burns the one holding it.

She spent years scorched by her own silence, blistered by the unspoken, wounded not by the cruelty of others but by her inability to speak her own truth.

Her first taste of wildfire came through the men she loved too deeply, too earnestly, too soon. They saw her softness and mistook it for fragility. They saw her compassion and mistook it for obedience. They saw her survival and mistook it for dependence. One by one, they tried to control her flame, dim it, own it. And every time they failed; they punished her for her brightness. She became familiar with men who wanted her warmth but not her power. Men who adored her light until they realized how hot it could burn. Men who loved the idea of her but panicked when they saw the truth of her fire.

Amelia learned something devastating during those years:

Some men don't want to love you they want to extinguish you.

But her flame, stubborn and sacred, refused to die. Even in her darkest moments, it sizzled quietly under her ribs, waiting watching preparing for the day she would finally stop shrinking and choose herself.

The day she would stop being afraid of her fire.

The day she would realize she had been fire all along.

•••

Her twenties became a battleground knifed open between her wildness and the world's expectations. It was the decade where she walked barefoot across the fault lines of her own becoming, where she tried to negotiate peace between her flame and the people who kept trying to smother it. She wanted to be loved, yes—but not at the cost of her heat. She wanted connection without confinement, intimacy without cages. Yet somehow, she kept ending up with men who were drawn to her fire the way moths are drawn to porch lights—hypnotized by the glow, but terrified once they felt the temperature. One man called her "too fiery," as if passion was an illness she should medicate. Another said she was "too loud," mistaking her reclaimed voice for rebellion. A third accused her of being "too passionate," as though intensity was a flaw instead of a language etched into her DNA. She didn't know then what she understands now: fire is a mirror. People reveal themselves when they stand near it. Some become warm. Some become terrified. Some become violent.

She fell for one man who worshiped her flame at first the way she spoke truth without trembling, the way she refused to shrink for anyone, the way her presence filled a room like heat rising from summer pavement. He told her her fire was powerful. He told her her freedom was intoxicating. He told her her strength made him better. But the moment her flame illuminated his insecurities, the worship twisted. His admiration curdled into jealousy. His affection sharpened into control. His voice chilled into commands. His hands became warnings. It was like loving a man-shaped shadow—one moment comfort, the next, darkness swallowing light.

The night he threatened her life was the night the truth detonated. She saw it not in his eyes, but in the way he trembled before her strength. He wasn't afraid of losing her he was afraid of what she looked like without him. Afraid she was brighter on her own. Afraid she was bigger without his shadow on her skin. Afraid she was fire he could no longer contain.

That night, her flame rose like a prophecy.
Not a wildfire. Not a frantic spark. But something older, deeper an ancestral heat that remembered every woman in her lineage who had swallowed her own light to survive.

She remembered none of the drive, only the terror. The red lights he ignored. The way the world blurred past the windows like smears of burning oil. The way his voice said, "If I can't have you, nobody will," with a finality that tasted like smoke. When she awakened on the side of the freeway, her nose broken, her face bleeding, and her breath shaking like a loose shutter in the wind, the sky above her looked too still. Too quiet. Too shocked to understand what had just happened. Her body trembled. Her vision swam. Her spirit staggered—but her flame... her flame refused to die.

It flickered stubbornly behind her ribs, glowing through the ache, the horror, the blood. And she whispered, through chapped, trembling lips, through pain that tasted like iron and memory:

"I live. I don't die. Not for you." Her words were not a scream. Not even a cry. They were a spark. A vow. A resurrection. In that moment, she remembered who she was.

Not water drowning. Not wind running. Fire returning.

In the aftermath, Amelia moved differently not loudly, not dramatically, but with a quiet heat that made the air shift when she entered a room. People couldn't explain it, but they felt it: the way she carried herself like a woman who had walked through flames and learned how to glow without burning herself. Her voice softened, but it also sharpened; every word had weight now, like iron pulled from a forge. Her boundaries tightened like the seams of a well-stitched garment. Her intuition once a whisper she doubted now rang through her like a bell at dawn. She no longer apologized for her intensity or tried to fold herself into smaller shapes to soothe other people's insecurities. She stopped dimming her flame to make others comfortable. She stopped allowing insecure men to warm their hands at her fire while insulting the heat that kept them alive. Choosing herself became her daily ritual not perfect, not flawless, but consistent, like sunrise.

She began to understand something the younger version of her never had language for: fire is not destruction unless someone tries to cage it. Fire, when allowed to move freely, becomes illumination. It becomes guidance. It becomes ceremony, cleansing the old to make space for the new. It becomes rebirth, the quiet phoenix inside every wounded woman. Amelia's fire transformed into the truth she could no longer swallow. It rose through her chest like a sun she'd hidden for too many years. It became the words she used to cut herself free from generational silence. It became the warmth she offered intentionally precious and selective to people who deserved her presence. It became the heat that burned away her shame, melted her doubt, softened her guilt, and chased the shadows of fear out of the corners of her spirit.

She learned she was both candlelight and wildfire gentle when loved correctly, ferocious when crossed, and always capable of rising from her own ashes. Her flame had layers now: flickers of tenderness, sparks of truth, blazes of conviction. She realized she didn't need to prove her fire; she only needed to protect it. And something miraculous happened in this new chapter of her becoming wind no longer worked against her flame. The wind that once rattled her windows and whispered warnings in childhood now moved with her, not around her. It carried her truth farther. It carried her courage wider. It carried her healing into rooms she once trembled to enter.

She became a woman whose fire did not ask for permission. A woman whose light did not shrink beneath doubt. A woman who walked with wind at her back and flame in her chest steady, certain, unextinguishable.

Wind gave breath to her flame.

Wind whispered, Burn anyway.

She no longer feared the fire inside her.
She became it.

Now, when Amelia speaks, her words don't simply fall into the air they *sizzle*. They crackle with conviction, like sparks leaping from a log just before it bursts into flame. Her voice rings with the weight of someone who has been silenced before and refuses to be again. There is a timbre to her now, a warmth and an edge, like a forge that has learned how to shape steel without losing its glow. She knows her fire can heal the way she comforts friends with a tenderness that feels like standing near a hearth on a cold night, the way she pours warmth into others with sincerity thick enough to melt their walls. But she also knows her fire can destroy the way she slices through manipulation like a torch cutting rope, the way her presence burns through lies until truth is the only thing left standing, the way she refuses to let disrespect slide into her life unnoticed or unanswered ever again.

Her story is not a tragedy. It is an ignition.
Every version of her that died did not vanish they cleared space, like old brush burning away so new roots could breathe. Every heartbreak ventilated her soul, letting out the smoke that had suffocated her lungs for too long. Every betrayal fanned her transformation like oxygen feeding a phoenix's wings. Every loss was a match struck in the dark, illuminating a path she once feared to walk alone. She understands now that her fire is both inheritance and rebellion an inheritance from the women before her who swallowed their flames to survive, and a rebellion against that very silence. It is her refusal to shrink the way her mother did. Her refusal to let fear choose her temperature. Her refusal to let the world decide when she is allowed to glow.

She is fire in its sacred form: warmth when the world grows cold, truth when lies try to cloud the air, rebirth when life demands evolution, illumination when the path grows dim, rage when boundaries are crossed, creation when everything else has felt like ash. She moves like a flame that knows her own power steady, living, alive with purpose. People feel her presence before she speaks now, the way one senses heat before seeing the flame. She has become her own sunrise, rising from horizons she once thought were endings. She has become the ember that refuses to go out. She has become the fire that finally, undeniably, belongs to her.

She stands now at the beginning of a new tale, her flame steady, her spirit uncontained, as if the world has finally stepped back enough to let her blaze in her full shape. There is a glow to her now that no one can deny a heat that lingers in the room even after she's walked away. When Amelia looks in the mirror, she no longer sees the trembling girl who swallowed her heat just to survive, who dimmed herself to make others comfortable, who hid her brilliance beneath the ashes of fear. She sees the woman who learned to rise from burning things, the way wildflowers grow through the charred soil of last season's fire. She sees the blaze that once terrified her steady now, familiar, loyal. She sees a power she no longer hides, a fire that no longer apologizes for its reach.

And when she speaks, her truth does not whisper it sizzles. It cracks like kindling catching flame. It sings in the air like metal meeting heat. It scorches silence the way lightning splits an old sky. Her voice is no longer timid; it carries the unmistakable cadence of someone who has walked through her own inferno and come out jeweled in resilience.

She says, with the certainty of a flame that knows its purpose: "I've been both candlelight and wildfire."

Candlelight gentle enough to guide children through nightmares, soft enough to soothe grief.

Wildfire powerful enough to burn through generational silence, unstoppable enough to clear paths for her future self.

She says, with a quiet fierceness:

"Healing in one hand.

Destruction in the other.

But finally both in my control."

Her fire is no longer reactive; it is intentional. It is the flame she cups in her palms, the light she chooses to carry, the heat she releases only for those worthy of its warmth. She understands now what she could not comprehend as a child: when fire is claimed, it becomes destiny. Not recklessness. Not ruin. But transformation.

And Amelia finally knows deep in her bones, deep in her breath, deep in the ancient flame inside her chest:

She is not the flames that hurt her.

She is the fire that saves her.

She is the spark that survived drowning.

She is the ember that refused to go out.

She is the blaze that rose in the darkness and lit her own path
forward.
And this this moment, this story, this awakening
is only the beginning of her burn.

Elemental Love
The Wounds & The Healing

You didn't meet the version of me
that was easy to love.
You met the version shaped by storms
the girl who learned early
that love was something you survived,
not something you trusted.

I came to you carrying oceans.
Not calm ones
the kind that drags broken things to shore
because they don't know where else to put them.

But you stayed.
Not to rescue me
but to witness me
the way no one ever had.

You listened to the tremble in my voice
the way some people listen to prayer.
You held my silence
like it was something valuable,
not something strange.

And slowly...
I softened.
Not because you asked me to
but because your presence
felt like the first warm day
after a long, brutal winter.

You became my Earth
steady, patient,
the grounding I didn't know I needed.
You held space for the pieces of me
I was terrified to reveal,
and still said,
"I'm not leaving."

Our Fire came quietly at first
like a spark we both felt
but didn't name out loud.
Then it grew
into warmth,
into longing,
into truth.

You touched me like you understood
that my body remembered pain
but was still capable of joy.
You kissed me like healing
was something I could taste.

And then came Wind
the freedom that frightened me
because freedom had always meant loss.
But you taught me that real love
doesn't clip wings.
It opens windows.

I learned to breathe with you.
To hope with you.
To dream with you.

Now here we are
Earth, Water, Fire, Wind
not perfect,
but present.
Not healed,
but healing.

Not unbroken,
but unafraid.

Loving you didn't save me.
It reminded me
that I was always worth saving.

Transition: The Doorway to Fire

Leaving him didn't happen with a scream.
It happened with a spark.
A single, trembling moment of clarity where Amelia felt her flame rise not wildly, not recklessly, but with the steady certainty of dawn pushing back the night. It was the first time she had heard her fire speak in years, not as panic, not as rage, but as truth. A calm, unwavering truth that said:
"Go."
She left him the way a wildfire steps out of smoke quietly, purposefully, with the kind of resolve that comes only from surviving what should have destroyed you. She gathered what little she owned, items that felt more like fragments than belongings, tucked her bruised spirit into a bag that once held softer dreams, and walked out without looking back.
Her footsteps sounded like embers cracking beneath her soles, tiny pops of heat breaking open the silence. The hallway felt too long, the night too still, but each step away from him felt like oxygen entering starved lungs. Her breath deepened. Her shoulders lifted. Her flame steadied.
The door didn't slam it sighed.
As if even the walls exhaled in relief.
As if the house itself knew it had held too much darkness, too much shadow, too much bruise.
Amelia stepped out into the world with a broken nose, blood dried at the corner of her lip, and a trembling body that felt stitched together by sheer will. But beneath all the hurt, her flame her stubborn, defiant flame still glowed under her ribs like a coal refusing to die. The trauma had carved her open, but in the hollow spaces left behind, something new began to move. Something ancient. Something brave. Something that remembered it was made of fire.
The air outside was cold, but she felt heat rising inside her, moving through her veins like a promise. She didn't yet know she was stepping into

herself. She didn't yet know she had just walked out of a grave disguised as a relationship. She didn't yet know the universe had cracked open a path for her.

She only knew this: she was alive.

And her fire shaken, flickering, wounded was still burning.

She didn't know it yet, but with every heartbeat, every inhale, every tender, painful step forward, she was walking toward a doorway. A threshold only fire could guide her through. A new chapter of her becoming. A calling she had been too afraid to answer until now.

She was walking toward Zora.

Toward the flame that would recognize her.

Toward the woman whose fire would not compete with hers but awaken it.

Toward the moment heat would meet heat and neither would have to shrink.

She was walking toward the very thing she had been running from her whole life: **herself**.

Healing didn't come as a straight line.

It arrived in sparks.

Some days, Amelia felt like smoke thin, drifting, barely holding shape. Other days, she felt like ash heavy, colorless, stripped of oxygen. But beneath it all, a new flame pulsed, small but certain. She fed it slowly. A journal entry here. A morning walk there. Long showers where she let water carry away old versions of herself. Nights wrapped in silence that no longer frightened her because she was learning to hear her own breath again.

In this tender chapter, she rebuilt herself piece by piece softly, patiently, sacredly.

Little did she know that somewhere across the city, another fire was waiting.

A flame that didn't want to consume her but recognize her.

Amelia began to move differently not like a woman running from something, but like a flame stepping into its rightful shape. Her energy shifted. People felt her before she spoke, as if the air grew warmer when she entered a room. Strangers asked her where she found her light. Friends studied her with quiet awe. Opportunities began to gravitate toward her like moths to warm glow.

She wasn't trying to impress anyone.
She was simply burning honestly.
Her fire drew people the way sunrise draws the horizon naturally, inevitably.
And that was when the universe placed her in the path of someone whose fire matched hers.

She saw Zora Mayfield before she ever heard her.
A silhouette in a dim-lit open mic, her posture a flame in human form upright, unbothered, unbreakable. Even standing still, Zora radiated heat. It rolled off her like summer pavement warm, alive, mesmerizing.
When Zora stepped onto the stage, Amelia felt the air shift. Felt her breath catch. Felt the space between them tighten like two sparks realizing they came from the same storm. Zora's presence didn't enter the room... it *ignited* it.
And then Zora spoke.
Her words did not wander; they struck.
They landed like fire on dry wood clean, bright, undeniable.
Amelia felt her chest open, her own flame rising in recognition.
Not competition.
Not intimidation.
Recognition.
As if her fire whispered inside her ribs:

Zora's eyes found her in the crowd, and for a split second, neither looked away. It wasn't attraction. It wasn't curiosity. It was energy recognizing itself like twin flames from different worlds suddenly aligned.
Their connection was instantaneous, quiet, electric.
A collision without impact.
Heat meeting heat.

After the show, Amelia lingered near the hallway, pretending to check her phone, pretending not to feel the pull happening inside her. Zora walked past, smelling like smoke and something honey sweet. She paused just slightly just enough for the universe to inhale.
"You write?" Zora asked, her voice warm, low, and edged with truth.
The question wasn't random.
It was recognition.
It was fire greeting fire.
Amelia swallowed, feeling heat coil in her stomach.

"Yes," she said. "I do."

Zora studied her not the way people study appearances, but the way fire studies oxygen: curious, knowing, familiar.

"Your energy," Zora said, nodding toward her chest, "felt loud from the stage."

Amelia's breath hitched.

Her flame fluttered.

It wasn't fear.

It was awakening.

From that moment on, their friendship took shape like two flames leaning toward each other—strengthening, expanding, growing brighter when side by side. Zora didn't try to tame Amelia's fire. She encouraged it. Nourished it. Challenged it. And Amelia, for the first time, felt her flame welcomed instead of weaponized.

This was not the beginning of romance.

This was the beginning of recognition.

Of sisterhood.

Of soul alignment.

A flame meeting its reflection.

Fire finally finding a place it didn't have to shrink.

And Amelia, standing in the aftermath of survival, felt something she hadn't felt in years:

Free.

Seen.

Unbroken.

Burning.

Zora's Story
The Making Of A Flame

Before the world ever saw Zora Mayfield blaze across a stage, she was just a girl trying to survive the smoke of her childhood.

Her strength wasn't a choice it was an inheritance born from chaos.

She grew up in a house where the walls always smelled like something burning, not from fire, but from the slow decay of people she loved. A mother addicted to crack, a stepfather drifting through the days like a ghost fueled by whatever substance kept him numb. Zora learned early that addiction is its own kind of weather unpredictable, violent, always shifting and children are often the ones left outside in the storm.

She was still a child when life demanded she become a mother.

Small hands lifting babies onto hips.

Small shoulders carrying responsibilities meant for grown bodies.

Small feet running between rooms, checking pulses of siblings who slept too deeply.

She became the sun in a house full of darkness, the only source of warmth her siblings knew. She fed them with whatever she could find canned beans, corner-store noodles, crumbs she stretched into meals with imagination. She told them stories at night to drown out the sounds of arguments, breaking glass, and footsteps that meant danger. She protected them like a lioness who hadn't yet grown her teeth.

And when the house ran out of everything food, money, safety Zora did what children should never have to do:

She learned to survive the streets.

Selling drugs wasn't rebellion.

It was survival.

It was a child trying to keep other children alive.

The streets taught her a new language fast, sharp, dangerous. Men twice her age underestimated her because she was young, because she was skinny, because she was a girl. They didn't realize that fire burns hottest in small spaces, and Zora had been smoldering her whole life.

But fire in a world that thrives on darkness becomes a target.

Zora fell into abusive relationships the way wounded birds fall into open hands hoping for safety, landing in cages. She kept choosing men who saw her strength as a threat and her softness as something to devour. Men who loved her only when she was broken. Men who mistook her loyalty for permission. Men who had their own addictions and used her heart as collateral damage.

But the deepest wound came from her mother the person she kept trying to love even when it hurt.

Zora spent years trying to save a woman who chose drugs over her children. Years of chasing a mother-shaped shadow. Years of begging a ghost to return to her body. Loving someone drowning in addiction is like trying to hold water in your hands it slips through your fingers no matter how tightly you clench.

Then came the boyfriend who drank like the world existed only to drown him.

He loved her loudly and hurt her quietly.
Apologized with tears but struck with hands.
Promised change but delivered bruises.
And yet Zora stayed.
Not because she was weak,
but because she had always been the one who fixed broken things.
She didn't know yet that some things shatter on purpose.

Then came the pregnancy.
A spark of hope, a light inside her, a heartbeat that made her believe she could rewrite the story she was born into. She spoke to her belly at night, whispering promises she had never heard herself. She planned a future where her child wouldn't grow up in chaos. Where she'd break every cycle that tried to break her.
But her boyfriend's rage didn't soften.
And the beatings grew.
And the bottle stayed full.
And one night, he didn't stop.
The loss of her baby carved a canyon through Zora's soul a grief that never healed straight.
It was the moment her flame shifted.
Not extinguished.
Shifted.
She learned then that pain can hollow you out, but it can also become a furnace.
Zora rose from that grief not as a survivor, but as something forged.
Fire doesn't apologize for burning when it has spent its whole life trying to keep others warm.
By the time Amelia meets her, Zora is the kind of flame people stare at powerful, mesmerizing, impossible to ignore. But behind the blaze is a history written in ash, smoke, and embers that refused to die.
Zora Mayfield didn't become fire.
She *was* fire
born from turmoil,
shaped by loss,
hardened by survival,
and destined to ignite every soul brave enough to stand near her

How Zora Found Poetry As Her Salvation

Poetry didn't enter Zora's life gently.
It didn't knock.
It didn't introduce itself.
It broke in like a burglar stealing her silence and leaving truth in its place.
She found it on a night when the world felt too heavy to carry.
Her mother was gone again lost somewhere between a high and a promise.
Her siblings were scattered between relatives' houses like forgotten pages in a torn book.
Her boyfriend had vanished into a liquor bottle, leaving bruises blooming like dark flowers on her arms.
And grief sharp, fresh, merciless grief still clawed at her womb from the child she had lost.
Zora stumbled into her own emptiness and sat on the bathroom floor, her back pressed against cold tile, trying to breathe through a pain that felt too big for her body.
And then without thinking, without planning, without permission,
words began pouring out of her.
Not spoken. Not whispered. Written.

Her hands found an old receipt on the floor, a pen from her stepfather's coat, and she scribbled the first poem of her life onto something meant to be thrown away.
It wasn't pretty. It wasn't polished. It was raw sharp as broken glass, trembling as a fresh wound, messy as her childhood. But it was *hers*. Her truth. Her heat. Her survival. The words came out of her like smoke leaving a burning house. Word after word. Line after line. Until the weight inside her chest loosened, until the shaking in her hands stopped, until the fire inside her felt less destructive and more like… **release.** That night, Zora realized something life-changing:

Her pain was trying to speak.
Her heart just didn't know the language until poetry came.

From that moment forward, writing became her ritual. Her refuge. Her rebellion. She wrote in stairwells. On bus stops. On the backs of food stamps and eviction notices. On napkins from fast-food restaurants where she hid from the chaos of home. In notebooks she borrowed and never returned. Her poems became the family she wished she had holding her, seeing her, surviving with her.

Poetry was the one place she could bleed without apologizing for the mess.

It gave her back all the things that life had taken:

A voice.

A spine.

A purpose.

A way to make meaning out of madness.

She stopped running from her fire and started writing it into shape. She turned her trauma into testimony. Her scars into scripture. Her heartbreak into heat.

And when she finally stepped onto a stage years later, the first time her voice echoed into a microphone, something ancient inside her unfurled.

The audience wasn't just listening they were *witnessing*. They were watching a girl made of smoke and grief transform into a woman made of flame. Poetry didn't save Zora in a soft way.

It saved her the way fire saves a frozen body by burning everything numb until life returns.

It didn't heal her instantly. It didn't erase her grief. But it gave her breath when life had stolen her lungs.

It gave her truth when silence had smothered her. It gave her a place to lay down her pain without fear of being judged or punished. Zora didn't choose poetry. Poetry chose her the way fire chooses dry wood, the way storms choose open sky, the way survival chooses the strongest heart in the room.

And from that moment on, she became the poet whose presence was a blaze, whose words were matches, whose voice could set a room on fire and leave people warmed, awakened, changed.

Poetry didn't just save Zora. It rebirthed her.

How Zora's Fire Sharpened into Leadership, Confidence & Presence

Zora didn't wake up one morning and decide to be a leader. Life carved her into one.

Her fire sharpened in the same way blades do through pressure, through friction, through being struck against what tried to dull her.

Poetry was the first place she learned she was powerful, but life was the furnace that shaped her. She grew confident the way flames grow in a fireplace: contained at first, controlled, testing their own strength, then rising higher once they learn they will not be snuffed out. Her presence became undeniable. People felt her before she stepped into a room a shift in temperature, a stir in the air, as if something alive, hot, and intentional had arrived.

She didn't command attention she **earned** it just by surviving.

Zora learned to speak with the authority of someone who had watched her world burn and still learned how to glow. She spoke with a spine forged from loss, with a voice strengthened by years of silence she refused to return to. She had once been a child who had to be everything— protector, provider, mother, soldier. Now she was a woman who refused to be anything less than direct, honest, and aligned with her truth. Her confidence wasn't loud or showy.

It was a **steady flame** the kind that warms, the kind that guides, the kind that outlasts the night.

People gravitated toward her because she radiated safety wrapped in fire. Her leadership wasn't about being the strongest person in the room it was about being the one who had already walked through hell and could tell everyone else where the exits were.

When she spoke, she didn't waste breath. Her words had weight, density, heat. Her voice no longer shook other people's voices did when they stood in the truth of her presence. She became the kind of woman others trusted without knowing why because fire recognizes fire, because survivors recognize survivors, because truth recognizes truth.

Women sat beside her and felt understood.

Men approached her and felt exposed.

Her siblings looked up to her as if she had hung the sun herself.

Zora learned to walk with her chin high not because she was arrogant, but because she had already lived through the kinds of things people swore would break her. She had learned to turn her lessons into lanterns, held high for others still stumbling in the dark.

Her fire sharpened into leadership each time she refused to dim herself to comfort someone insecure. It sharpened into confidence each time she said no without justification.

It sharpened into presence each time she chose healing over habit.
Even her silence carried power.
A quiet heat.
An unspoken message that said:
"I know who I am now.
I know what I survived.
And I will not make myself small for anyone."
Zora no longer needed validation, permission, or applause.
She had become her own flame
self-lit, self-fed, self-sustaining.
She didn't seek to lead.
She simply led by existing as someone who refused to be
extinguished.
People followed her because she burned with the kind of clarity
that only comes from rising out of ashes not once, but over and over again.
Her fire wasn't wild anymore.
It was **focused**.
It was **intentional**.
It was **hers**.
And that presence—steady, fierce, undeniable—is exactly what
Amelia felt the moment their paths crossed.

The Night Amelia First Sees Zora Perform

The Ember Lounge breathed like a living thing—warm, low,
pulsing with bodies and bass. The lights were dim, tinted the color of
bruised sunsets. Incense curled through the air like wandering spirits.
Conversations hummed like soft electricity. It was a place where broken
people came to bleed beautifully and whole people came to remember
their cracks.
Amelia sat toward the back, her heart still tender, her fire still
learning to stand. She didn't know why she came—only that something
pulled her here, something warm and steady, like fate lighting a match.
Then the host stepped onto the stage.
He cleared his throat.
He smirked a little.
He said one name:

"Zora Mayfield."

And the room changed.

A hush rippled across the space, that rare kind of silence where even the air holds its breath. Heads turned. Conversations cut off. Even the lights seemed to shift, as if they, too, wanted a better view.

Then Zora walked out.

She didn't enter the stage

she ignited it.

Tall, striking, carved from survival and sunlight, she moved like a flame learning its own choreography. Her hair, wild and natural, framed her like a halo made of fire. Her gold hoops caught the light. Her posture was a poem all by itself—chin high, shoulders relaxed, a quiet power radiating off her in steady waves.

Amelia felt her chest tighten.

Not in fear.

In recognition.

Zora stood at the mic, letting silence fill the room like oxygen before a spark. Her presence warmed the space before she even spoke.

And then her voice.

Low.

Smooth.

Sharp.

Like honey poured over broken glass.

She didn't read her poem.

She embodied it.

Her voice carried the cadence of someone who had swallowed storms and spit out lightning. Every word dropped heavy, like embers landing on dry earth. The room leaned forward—every head, every heart like worshippers bowing to a new kind of altar.

Zora spoke of growing up in a house where addiction was the family heirloom.

Where she mothered children, she didn't give birth to.

Where she fed siblings from empty cabinets.

Where she survived men who mistook her light for a fire they could control.

And as she spoke, it didn't feel like a poem.

It felt like truth unzipped.

Like soul tissue laid bare.

Like fire remembering it was fire.

People snapped their fingers, but softly, afraid to interrupt the spell.

Amelia felt every line down her spine like a match striking bone. She saw her own pain reflected in Zora's rhythm.

She felt her own flame rise with each confession Zora released into the room.

Then Zora paused, looking out over the audience as if searching for something she had lost long ago. Her gaze swept the room like a lighthouse and then stopped.

On Amelia.

It was only a second.

But it felt like a collision.

Fire meeting fire.

Heat recognizing heat.

Two stories cut from different wounds but stitched with the same flame.

Then Zora spoke her final lines soft but lethal:

> **"I learned to hold myself**
> **the way fire holds light**
> **without apology.**
> **Without fear.**
> **Without asking anyone**
> **for permission to burn."**

Silence.

Thick.

Sacred.

Almost holy.

Then the room erupted snaps, shouts, stomps, applause that filled the air with electricity. But Zora didn't bask in it. She stepped away from the mic with the calm grace of someone who had nothing to prove.

She walked offstage the way she walked on:

blazing.

Amelia couldn't move.

Her breath lodged in her throat; her pulse unsteady.

Something inside her had shifted

cracked open

risen.

Her fire had found its mirror.

Where Fire Meets Fire
Amelia & Zora — Two Flames, Two Histories, One Heat

There are many ways to be fire.

Two women can burn and never scorch the same way. Two flames can rise from different storms, different wounds, different worlds and still recognize each other instantly.

This is how the universe works. This is how fire moves. This is how Amelia and Zora found each other. Side by side, they were not the same flame but they were born of the same element.

Amelia's Fire

The flame that learned to whisper before it learned to roar. Amelia's fire was quiet at first, a shy glow tucked deep beneath her ribs, trying to stay lit in a house full of storms.

She grew up tiptoeing around explosions that weren't hers arguments that cracked walls, slammed doors that shook ceilings, silence that pressed against her like winter frost.

Her flame flickered through childhood like the smallest of candles delicate, hidden, soft enough to be mistaken for weakness. Her fire grew inside water. Inside drowning. Inside survival.

Her heat came from learning to rise after sinking, finding breath under pressure, rebuilding herself from the inside out. Amelia's flame is **gentle**, but never fragile. It is the quiet burn the ember that refuses to die, the sunrise flame that grows slowly until it blinds you with its warmth. Her fire heals. Her fire warms. Her fire protects. Her fire grows brighter the more she loves. She is candlelight turned wildfire but only, when necessary, only when crossed, only when survival becomes truth.

Zora's Fire

The flame that roared before anyone thought to listen. Zora's fire was born loud, a blaze ignited in a house where chaos was language and neglect was routine.

She grew up feeding siblings instead of playing with dolls.

She wiped tears from children's faces before learning how to wipe her own.

She walked through rooms filled with addiction, broken promises, and adults who treated responsibility like something to snort, swallow, or ignore.

Her flame grew inside smoke.

Inside scarcity.

Inside her own grit.

While Amelia silently negotiated with storms, Zora learned to be the storm the heat that fought back, the blaze that protected, the fire that refused to be consumed. Her fire is **fierce**, unapologetic, unhidden.

It speaks in crackles and sparks, in truth that can scorch, in presence that cannot be dimmed. Zora's fire does not whisper. It demands space. It refuses to shrink. It refuses to die.

She is wildfire turned candlelight only when she chooses, only for those who have earned her tenderness.

Two Flames, Side By Side

Amelia burns inward.
Zora burns outward.
Amelia is the flame that warms from within.
Zora is the flame that lights the whole room.
Amelia's heat is healing.
Zora's heat is cleansing.
Amelia grew fire in darkness.
Zora grew fire in daylight.
Amelia learned to survive water.
Zora learned to survive smoke.
Amelia's flame glows like morning sun
gentle, patient, steady.
Zora's flame blazes like desert heat
bold, unfiltered, relentless.
But fire is fire
and when two flames recognize each other,
they don't extinguish.
They rise.
Where Amelia is softness holding power,
Zora is power choosing softness.

Where Amelia carries strength shaped by silence,
Zora carries strength sharpened by noise.
Where Amelia learned to speak slowly,
Zora learned to speak loudly.

But together
together they become balance,
equilibrium,
light and heat,
sunrise and bonfire.

The Moment Fire Met Fire

When Amelia saw Zora on stage,
she recognized something she'd never seen outside her own chest
a flame that survived everything designed to extinguish it.
Zora recognized something too
the familiar glow of someone who fought their own shadows
and came out lit from the inside.
Two women.
Two fires.
Two histories written in ash.
Different beginnings.
Different burn.
Same language.
When their eyes met across the room,
the universe knew what it was doing.
Destiny flickered.
Energy collided.
Heat rose.
They didn't compete.
They didn't clash.
They simply **recognized**.

Amelia thought,
"She burns like I feel."
Zora thought,
"That one has fire in her."

That's how flames speak to each other.
Without words.
Without touch.
Without explanation.
Just heat recognizing heat.
And in that moment,
the world witnessed two stories
two women
two fires
finding not their match,
but their **mirror**.

The Night Fire Spoke

The Ember Lounge felt alive that night alive in the way only a place built from heartbreak and art can be. The air shimmered with incense and neon shadows. The walls hummed with old poems and new beginnings. Every table flickered with candlelight that danced like restless spirits. It was the kind of place where people came to hear their own souls echoed back to them.

Amelia slipped into the back corner, her flame still tender, still rebuilding, still unsure of its strength. She didn't know why she came. Something had tugged her here, something warm and insistent, like the universe whispering, *You need to see this.*

And then the host stepped up to the mic, smiled a knowing smile, and said one name that changed everything:

"Give it up for... Zora Mayfield."

A hush fell so fast it felt physical, like someone pressed pause on the entire room.

Zora walked onto the stage the way fire enters a room.

Not to destroy, but to **announce itself**.

She carried herself with the ease of someone who had survived her own apocalypse and returned wiser. Her aura was heat. Her presence was gravity. People sat up straighter without meaning to.

Her hair, wild and untamed, framed her like a burning crown.

Her posture said: *I bend for no one.*

Her silence said: *Listen carefully.*

Even the candles seemed to glow brighter in her presence.

Amelia felt her heartbeat trip over itself.

•••

When Zora Spoke, the Air Shifted

Zora stepped up to the mic, her fingers brushing it with the reverence of someone about to confess a truth that costs part of the soul to speak.

Then her voice—low, velvety, sharp—cut through the room like a blade warmed in flame.

She told a poem about her childhood, where addiction slept in the walls and chaos ate at the foundation. She spoke about feeding siblings with hands too small to carry that much responsibility. She confessed to selling drugs not for rebellion but for survival. She told the room about loving a mother who chose the high over hugs, about losing a child to a man's violence, about learning to breathe again after heartbreak threatened to bury her alive.

The audience didn't just listen, they *felt* her.

Each line was a flame.

Each pause was smoke rising.

Each truth was a spark landing on tender hearts.

Amelia felt every word burn into her, carving space, making room, lighting her from the inside out. Her chest ached. Her throat tightened. Her own fire stirred, restless, awakened by the echo of someone who burned the way she did.

Zora didn't perform.

She released.

She erupted.

She rose.

Her voice carried every wound, every triumph, every resurrection. She wasn't just telling a story, she was offering the room warmth from a fire she built with her own pain.

And then, mid-poem, her eyes found Amelia.

The Collision

For a moment
the world stilled.
The crowd blurred.
The candles paused their dance.
Even the music from outside evaporated.
It was just two flames staring across a room,
recognizing each other in an instant.
Amelia's breath caught.
Zora's voice softened—barely, but enough.
Heat rose between them, not romantic, not dangerous,
a recognition.
A knowing.
A meeting of elements.
Amelia thought:
She burns like truth.
Zora thought:
That one has fire in her.
It was as if the universe said,
"Here. This one. You two need each other."
And they did.

Zora finished her poem with final lines that felt directed
at Amelia alone:
> **"I learned to hold myself**
> **the way fire holds light**
> **without apology,**
> **without fear,**
> **without asking anyone**
> **for permission to burn."**

Silence.
Then applause that shook the glasses on the tables.
But Amelia didn't clap.
She couldn't move.
Something inside her had cracked open,
not broken,
but awakened.

The First Conversation
Where Fire Meets Flame

Backstage at The Ember Lounge was dim, narrow, and warm the kind of warmth that clings to the skin and carries whispers of every performance that happened before. The walls were covered in posters of poets long gone; their signatures faded like old fingerprints. A single bulb flickered above the dressing mirror, glowing like a tired star.

Zora stepped into the hallway still glowing from her performance, her energy buzzing like heat shimmering on asphalt. A few performers congratulated her as she passed, but she brushed off the praise with the ease of someone who had learned not to measure her worth by applause.

As she moved toward the dressing room, she felt it again: that heat she'd sensed while on stage. A warmth rising off someone like a whisper of flame.

She turned her head.

And there stood Amelia.

Pressed against the wall, hands folded, eyes wide.

Not with fear, but with recognition.

Zora slowed, then stopped.

How Zora Approaches Amelia

Zora wasn't the type to chase energy she drew it. But something about Amelia's presence tugged at her like a soft rope around her ribs. She walked up to her, not forcefully, not casually

but with the kind of certainty only fire has when it knows it has found another spark.

"Hey," Zora said, voice low, warm, still vibrating with leftover stage heat. "You were in the back, right?"

Amelia nodded, though her throat felt too tight to speak.

Zora smirked gently the kind of smirk that says *I see you even if you don't speak.*

"I felt your energy," she continued. "From the stage."

Amelia's breath hitched.

Zora saw it.

"Most people just watch," Zora said. "You... felt."

"That poem…" Amelia whispered. "It felt like… like you were speaking my story."

Zora leaned in slightly, her voice low, warm. "That's because fire recognizes fire. You feel me because you *are* me."

A shiver rolled up Amelia's spine.

Not fear, alignment.

From that moment, something unspoken settled between them not friendship yet, but the beginning of one.

A trust born from shared heat.

A bond made of flame, not obligation.

Two women from different worlds.

Two survivors.

Two flames rising in their own time.

That night, Zora and Amelia didn't just meet.

They **found** each other.

And the world

without knowing

shifted just a little.

Amelia's Inner Monologue

Why does she feel familiar?
Why do I feel seen?
Why does this woman speak like she knows the parts of me
I've buried?
My heart won't slow down.
Her aura is heat… steady heat…
like the first warm day after winter.
Why can't I look away?
Is this what recognition feels like?
Is this what destiny sounds like walking up to you in human form?
She burns with truth.
She burns with purpose.
She burns with things I am only just learning to claim.

Zora's Inner Monologue

She has a flame in her.
Not the loud kind
the deep kind.
The dangerous kind.
The kind that can burn a life open or light a new one.
She doesn't know her heat yet.
But I do.
I see it on her skin.
In her breath.
Behind her eyes.
That glow that trembling glow.
She's fire that's been put out too many times.
But she's rising again.
And she's drawn to my flame the way heat always calls to heat.

The Birth Of Their Friendship
Fire Choosing Fire

Zora crossed her arms and leaned against the opposite wall, studying Amelia the same way flames study oxygen—tentative, curious, wanting to know if it could breathe there.

"So," Zora said softly. "Do you write?"

Amelia swallowed.

"Yes. I... I do."

Zora nodded as if she'd known the answer before the question left her mouth.

"I could tell," she said. "Your energy was loud. Even your silence had heat."

Amelia blinked, stunned that someone could read her like that.

"You ever perform?" Zora asked.

Amelia shook her head. "Not anymore."

"Why?"

The question cut cleanly sharp but gentle, like a warm knife slicing through cold butter.

Amelia looked at the floor.

"I guess I forgot who I was," she whispered.

Zora stepped closer just one step, but it felt like a shift in the atmosphere, like the room itself expanded to make space for their connection.

"Then remember," Zora said.

"Because your fire is waking up. I felt it."

Amelia looked up, meeting Zora's gaze fully for the first time.

Zora held her eyes without blinking, without flinching, without looking away, the way only someone unafraid of fire can.

"Your story matters," Zora said. "Whether you tell it on a stage or whisper it into a journal, it matters. And you? You're not done burning yet."

Something in Amelia cracked open not in pain, but in release.

For the first time in a long time, she felt her flame stretching, rising, breathing.

"Thank you," Amelia whispered. Zora nodded, her expression softening.

"That's what fire does," she said. "We help each other stay lit."

There it was—the moment Fire chose Fire.

Not as rivals.

Not as teachers.

Not as saviors.

But as mirrors.

Two women who carried fire for different reasons,

who burned in different ways,

but who recognized in each other the rarest thing:

A flame that refused to die.

Zora's Dark Secret

Zora Mayfield lived her life like a flame trying to behave:

contained, intentional, disciplined.

She tried to stay away from the kind of heat that once burned her childhood into a battlefield:

Crime, chaos, violence, and all the ghosts she had spent years outrunning.

She wanted peace. She wanted order. She wanted a life where her fire illuminated instead of destroyed. But trouble had a way of recognizing its own. It followed her like smoke that clings to clothes no matter how many times you wash them.

No matter how good she tried to be, the streets the past always seemed to find her shadow.

On one particular afternoon, Zora and Amelia had been hanging out all day. Two flames, newly bonded, learning the rhythms of each other's heat.

They had no plans other than errands: the pharmacy, the grocery store, the bank.

Both were recovering from being laid off from a temp telemarketing job, a job that had ended in a way that felt more like a nightmare than a termination.

They never talked about that day.

The day they walked into the office and found their boss lying on the floor—eyes open, blood blooming across the carpet like a dark red flower.

It had been surreal, horrifying, and confusing. Zora had acted strangely, pacing, muttering under her breath, avoiding eye contact. Amelia thought it was trauma. Shock. Fear. But now...

Now the pieces were about to rearrange themselves into something more dangerous.

The Bank Window

The bank wasn't busy. Just a few people in line.
Amelia hummed softly, playing with her keys while Zora stepped up to the teller.

It should've been simple. Zora smiled politely, placed her ID on the counter, and said, "Just need to withdraw twenty from checking." The teller looked at the ID.

Then at Zora.

Then at the ID again. The air changed Amelia felt it immediately.

A shift.

A tightening.

A stillness that tasted like the moment right before something catches fire.

The teller's eyebrows knit together. "This ID..." she said slowly. "It's your photo... but the name is different." "Different how?" Amelia blurted, stepping closer.

The teller turned the ID slightly. The name read:
Zara Miller.

Not Zora Mayfield. Not even close. Zora's face went pale paler than Amelia had ever seen. Her mouth opened, then closed. Her eyes normally so sharp, so confident went wide, filled with wildfire panic. She snatched the ID back too quickly. Too defensively. "Thank you," she muttered. "We're good."

She grabbed Amelia's wrist and pulled her away from the counter, speed-walking across the lobby. They pushed through the glass doors into the parking lot, the sun hitting them like a slap.

"Zora, what is..."

"Not here."

Her voice was tight.

Almost trembling.

They got into the car, slammed the doors shut, and sat in thick, suffocating silence.

The Confession

Zora stared at the steering wheel as if debating whether to hold it or break it.

Finally, she spoke. "I need to tell you something."

Amelia said nothing.

She felt her own heart beating in her throat. She felt heat rising in her chest—the fire that warned her when something wasn't right. "My name..." Zora inhaled slowly. "My real name isn't Zora Mayfield." Amelia froze. "Zara Miller," Zora continued. "That was my birth name."

"Then why change it?" Zora exhaled sharply, her hands shaking. "Because I'm... I'm on the run, Amelia." The words dropped between them like a match onto gasoline. Amelia blinked.

"What do you mean, 'on the run'?" Zora looked at her with an expression Amelia had never seen—fragile, terrified, burning at the edges.

"There was an investigation," she whispered. "A murder investigation. And I was named a possible suspect."

Amelia felt the world tilt. Her stomach dropped. Her lungs tightened. "Our boss..." Zora continued. "The one we found. The man lying on the floor. Amelia... they questioned me about him before we ever got laid off." Amelia's breath turned sharp. Flashbacks flickered like old film reels Zora pacing the office when they found the body, Zora refusing to touch anything.

Zora insisting they leave before police came, Zora shaking so violently she couldn't even dial 911. At the time, Amelia thought trauma. Shock. Fear. But now now the pieces were rearranging themselves into something darker. "Why would they suspect you?" Amelia whispered.

Zora ran a hand down her face. "Because he knew things about my past… things I told him when I thought he was someone I could trust. And when he was killed… they found my name in his notes." Amelia's pulse hammered. "You didn't" "No," Zora said immediately, eyes blazing. "Amelia, I didn't kill him. I swear on my life. But I panicked. Because people like me? With my past? With my record? We don't get the benefit of the doubt. We get handcuffs."

She swallowed hard. "So I ran. Changed my name. Started over."

Amelia felt breathless.

Not from fear but from the weight of the truth. "Why didn't you tell me?" she asked softly.

Zora looked at her with eyes full of wildfire vulnerability. "Because you're the first person in a long time who made me feel… safe. Seen. Not judged. I didn't want to ruin that."

Amelia's flame rose not in anger, but in fierce empathy.

"Zora…" she whispered.

And for the first time since she'd known her, Zora's fire flickered.

Amelia's Inner Thoughts

It all makes sense now.
The way she moved that day.
The way she avoided touching things.
The panic.
The erratic breathing.
The fear hidden behind her fire.
But if I know anything about her…
anything at all…
it's that Zora burns from truth, not violence.
And yet…
this is danger.

Real danger.
And now I'm standing in it with her.

Zora's Inner Thoughts

She's going to leave.
I can feel it.
Everyone leaves when they see the parts of me I can't clean up,
the smoke I carry,
the heat I never asked for.
But she stayed this long...
maybe...
maybe she won't run.

The Bond
Fire Choosing Fire Again

Amelia reached out, placed her hand over Zora's.
Zora flinched
not from fear,
but from surprise.
"Listen to me," Amelia said, steady as sunrise.
"I believe you."
Zora's breath hitched.
"You do?"
"Yes," Amelia said.
"Because your fire doesn't lie. It burns too honestly."
Something in Zora broke open then,
not in weakness,
but in relief.
For the first time in years,
she wasn't running alone.
Fire had chosen fire
again.
And this time,
the flames intertwined.
Not to destroy.
But to survive.

The Clues Were Always There

Amelia had always loved true crime.
Not the sensational kind
but the human kind.
The kind that asked *Why?*
The kind that examined darkness to understand survival.
The kind that taught her patterns, motives, red flags—things her
childhood had never given her language for.
True crime was her comfort.
Her curiosity.
Her therapy.
Her way of making sense of a world that had often made no sense
to her.
She watched documentaries while cooking, listened to podcasts
while cleaning, fell asleep to narrators dissecting motives, timelines,
suspects.
Darkness didn't scare Amelia—
she had grown up in the shadows.
Knowing the shape of monsters helped her sleep better at night.
But Zora?
Zora always refused.
Whenever Amelia suggested a documentary,
Zora would tense slightly,
smile too quickly,
shake her head too firmly.
"Nah, I'm good on that."
or
"Girl, let's watch something lighter."
or
"I don't like that murder stuff."
Amelia would shrug, thinking nothing of it.
She thought Zora was just sensitive, or tired, or uninterested.
But now,
with the bank incident
and the confession
and the unraveling truth
everything began to rearrange itself
like puzzle pieces clicking into place.

The Realization

They sat in Amelia's living room after leaving the bank, silent except for the low hum of the refrigerator and the thick, pulsing presence of the truth.

Zora's hands were still shaking.

Amelia's mind was racing.

And then

like a match struck in the dark

Amelia remembered:

Zora never watched true crime with her.

A chill snaked up her spine.

Not fear—

recognition.

Flashbacks flickered like film reels:

- Late nights when Amelia suggested documentaries and Zora said, "Let's watch something else."
- The time Amelia put on a podcast and Zora left the room, claiming she needed to take a call.
- The time a Netflix thriller auto-played and Zora's breathing grew shallow, her knee bouncing.
- The night Amelia wanted to watch a series about fugitives and Zora visibly tensed, whispering, "Turn it off, please."

Amelia had never questioned it.

Never pushed.

Never asked why.

Because Zora was strong.

Fearless.

Fire in human form.

But now she saw the truth:

Zora didn't avoid true crime because she was squeamish.

She avoided it because she was living it.

She was the kind of woman true crime stories were written about

not the villain,

but the survivor caught in the wrong place,

the wrong time,

with the wrong shadows following her.

The Conversation

Amelia exhaled slowly.
"It all makes sense now," she whispered.
Zora looked up, eyes tired.
"What does?"
"The true crime stuff."
Zora blinked.
"What about it?"
"You never wanted to watch any of it," Amelia said softly.
"And I never understood why."
A heavy silence settled between them
the kind that admits truth before words do.
Zora swallowed hard.
"I couldn't," she said. "Every time I heard a story about running or suspects or police or... or murder..."
She wiped a tear before it fell. "It felt too close. Like I was watching my own ghost."
Amelia's chest tightened.
Zora shook her head slowly. "I didn't want you looking at me with the same eyes you look at those cases with. Didn't want you analyzing me. Didn't want you wondering."
"But I'm not wondering," Amelia said gently. "I believe you."
Zora's face crumpled with relief so raw it felt sacred.
"Amelia," she whispered, "I didn't do it."
"I know," Amelia said.
And she meant it.
With her whole flame.

Amelia's Inner Thoughts

The signs were there...
The flinches.
The avoidance.
The way she shut down when crime came on TV.
The way her breath changed when the news mentioned fugitives.
She wasn't hiding guilt—
she was hiding fear.

A fear that had shaped her life,
a fear she carried alone until now.
But now I see the whole picture.
She's not the monster.
She's the woman running from monsters.

Zora's Inner Thoughts

I thought she'd figure it out.

I thought she'd notice the way my chest tightened at every crime scene reenactment, the way my palms sweated when narrators talked about suspects going on the run, the way I left the room to avoid hearing words that felt like knives.

I thought she'd turn on me the moment she connected the dots.
But she's still here.
She's still looking at me with fire in her eyes,
not fear,
not judgment
fire.
Maybe for the first time...
I'm safe.

The Bond Deepens
Fire Chooses Fire Again

Amelia reached over and took Zora's hand.
"You don't have to hide from me," she said softly. "Not anymore."
Zora inhaled a shaky breath.
"You sure?"
"Positive."
Zora let out a breath she'd been holding for years, a release so deep it sounded like smoke leaving a burning house.
Amelia squeezed her hand.
"Besides," she said gently, "True crime always taught me one thing..."
Zora raised her eyes.
"And what's that?"

"That not everyone who runs is guilty. Some people run because the world won't listen to them."

Zora's eyes filled.

Not with fear.

Not with shame.

But with something warm.

Something ancient.

Something relieved.

Fire recognizing fire—in the deepest, darkest corner of survival.

The Night Zora's Fire Raged

They sat in Amelia's living room, the lamp casting a soft amber glow across Zora's trembling hands. Outside, the world moved on—cars passing, wind brushing against windows, life humming as usual.

But inside, something sacred was happening.

Something heavy.

Something that needed air.

Zora swallowed hard, eyes drifting toward the wall as though watching a memory replay itself in shadow.

"Amelia…" she said quietly. "There's more. About why I ran. About who I used to be."

Amelia's breath stilled, her flame tightening in her chest.

"Tell me," she whispered.

Zora closed her eyes.

And the truth began.

The Confession — Fire Unleashed

"I was tired," Zora murmured,

voice breaking like dry wood under pressure.

"Not just tired done.

Done being hit.

Done being threatened.

Done being someone's punching bag."

Her jaw clenched.

"I stayed with him longer than I should have. I thought… maybe he'd change. Maybe love was enough. Maybe if I loved him harder, he'd stop hurting me."

She shook her head slowly, bitterness simmering in her voice.

"But that night… that night was the last straw."

She took a shaky breath.

"He pushed me," she said. "Hard. Into a counter. I hit my head. And something inside me—something deep, something ancient, something I didn't even know I had—snapped."

Her eyes filled, not with weakness, but with the wildfire truth of a moment that changed everything.

"I felt the fire rise. Not anger. Rage. The kind that comes from years of swallowing your voice. The kind that comes from every bruise, every apology you shouldn't have made, every tear you cried in secret. It wasn't a spark—it was an eruption."

Her hands trembled.

"And before I knew it… I grabbed a kitchen knife."

The room grew still.

Even the air leaned in to listen.

"I blacked out," Zora whispered.

"I just remember the fire. The heat. The sound of my heart pounding louder than his yelling."

Her throat tightened.

"And when I came back… when I opened my eyes…"

She choked on the memory.

"There was blood everywhere, Amelia.

Everywhere."

Her voice cracked like burnt timber.

"My first thought wasn't even guilt. It was survival.

Run.

Because women like me don't get empathy.

We don't get understanding.

We get judged before we even open our mouths."

Amelia's eyes softened, filling with heat, empathy, truth.

The Cleanup — Fire Turned Instinct

Zora stared at her hands as though remembering the weight they had once carried.

"I don't know where the strength came from," she whispered. "Maybe adrenaline. Maybe fear. Maybe the fire inside me doing whatever it had to do to survive."

She wiped her eyes roughly.

"I cleaned up the blood.

Not perfectly—just enough.

Enough for panic to take over.

Enough for instinct to lead."

Her voice trembled.

"I hid the body."

The words hit the air like sparks landing on gasoline.

"I had never done anything like that before," she said, shaking her head as though still shocked by her own past.

"I didn't plan it. I didn't think. I just… moved. Like my body knew I had to disappear before the world came for me."

Her breath shuddered.

"I took his truck.

Drove through the night.

Straight to California.

To family who didn't ask questions.

I changed everything—my name, my address, my story."

A tear slid down her cheek.

"I didn't even mourn him. I mourned the woman I was before him. The girl who didn't know fire lived inside her. The girl who thought she deserved the pain."

Amelia's Inner Thoughts

She isn't a monster.
She is a woman the world pushed to the edge
and then blamed for falling.
She didn't burn out of malice
she burned out of survival.
And if I had lived her life…
would I have done anything different?

Zora's Inner Thoughts

This is the moment she leaves.
This is when she pulls away,
calls me dangerous,
calls me crazy,
runs for the door.
But she's still here.
Why is she still here?
Why isn't she afraid?

The Choice
Fire Stays With Fire

Amelia moved closer, placing her hand gently over Zora's.

Zora flinched, not from fear, but from not knowing how to be held during a confession this heavy.

"Look at me," Amelia whispered.

Zora lifted her eyes.

"What you went through… what he put you through… no human should suffer that. You didn't choose violence. Violence chose you. You just fought back."

A tear dropped onto Zora's hand.

"And I'm not leaving you," Amelia said.

"Not now.

Not after knowing everything.

Not ever."

Zora broke then

her face collapsing into her palms,

her sobs raw and quiet,

her fire flickering in the open air

for the first time without shame.

Amelia pulled her into an embrace, steady, warm, unwavering.

Two flames

one trembling,

one steady

burning together in the dark.

And for the first time,
Zora let someone hold her fire
without fearing she'd be burned.

The Doubt That Flickered

Amelia sat silently after Zora's confession, her fingers still wrapped around Zora's shaking hands.

The room was warm, but inside her chest something cold began to form—a tiny frost crawling across her flame.

Doubt.

Not loud.

Not accusatory.

Just a small, uneasy whisper at the back of her mind.

Zora's story was devastating, visceral, believable, filled with pain Amelia recognized, survival she respected,
fire she understood.

But something didn't sit right.

Something Zora wasn't saying.
Something she was keeping folded between her words like a secret she wasn't ready to unfold.

Amelia hated herself for even feeling it
but the truth was the truth:

She wasn't completely sure Zora had told her everything.

The Shift In The Room

Zora wiped her tears, breathing shakily, exhausted from the weight of all she had confessed.

And Amelia held her, but inside?

Her mind was racing,
the way wind swirls when it senses a storm coming.
She replayed the night they found their boss
the way Zora had acted,
the panic,
the urgency,
the insistence on leaving quickly,
the tremor in her voice that didn't sound like simple shock.

At the time, Amelia thought it was trauma.
But now...
Now the memory felt different.
Zora had claimed her violent past was tied to an ex who beat her.
She claimed she blacked out.
She claimed she ran from her old life, not from new accusations.
But the police had questioned her, multiple times,
even before the murder at their workplace.
And Amelia had seen Zora's face that day in the office—
the way her eyes darted,
the way she scanned the room like a hunted animal,
the way she refused to touch anything,
the way she whispered "We need to go. Now. Don't call anyone yet."
At the time, Amelia didn't question it.
But now?
Everything felt connected in a way that made Amelia's flame tremble.

Amelia's Inner Thoughts

What if she wasn't just running from her past...
but from something she still hasn't admitted?
What if the blackout wasn't the only time she lost control?
What if her fire—this powerful, fierce, unpredictable fire
had burned more than one person?
What if what happened to our boss wasn't random?
What if someone from her past followed her?
Or worse...
She swallowed hard, forcing the thought down.
What if Zora did have something to do with it...
and she's not telling me?

Zora's Inner Thoughts

(completely unaware of Amelia's shifting flame)
I told her everything—everything that matters.
I didn't tell her the rest.
Not yet.
Not until I know I can trust her with the whole truth.

But she stayed.
She held my hand.
Maybe... maybe I can tell her the rest soon.

The Moment Between Them

Amelia stood to pour Zora a glass of water, needing to move, needing breath to clear the fog in her mind. But when she turned back and saw Zora looking so small, so raw, so human...
Her heart softened.
Amelia handed her the glass.
Their fingers brushed.
Heat passed between them.
The familiar fire, the connection they'd built.
Zora whispered, "Thank you... for not leaving."
Amelia forced a smile, her voice gentle. "I'm here."
But inside her chest, her flame flickered uneasily.
Because she was there, but she wasn't sure for how long, or what she was standing in the middle of. And in that moment, Amelia realized something that made her breath tighten:
Fire recognizes fire...
but fire can also be deceiving.

The Seed Of Suspicion

As Zora leaned back into the couch, closing her eyes, Amelia watched her quietly.
And the thought she had been trying to avoid finally took shape:
What if our boss didn't die because of something random? What if trouble didn't follow Zora. What if it traveled with her?
Amelia didn't want to believe it.
She didn't want to imagine Zora capable of that kind of fire.
But she couldn't ignore the truth
Something wasn't adding up.
Not yet.
Not fully.
But the cracks had formed.
And now, Amelia's fire wasn't just curious, it was alert.
Watchful.

Cautious.
Two flames still touching, but no longer burning in perfect harmony.
Something was coming.
Something big.
And Amelia could feel it in her bones.

When The Past Broke Down The Door

The house was quiet.
Too quiet.
Zora sat on the couch, still trembling from her confession.
Amelia hovered nearby, pretending to straighten blankets,
pretending her heart wasn't beating like a trapped bird.
The air felt thick—
like the moment right before a storm shreds the sky open.
Amelia opened her mouth to speak
but she never got the chance.
Because suddenly
BOOM.
A violent crash shook the entire living room.
The front door slammed inward,
splintering,
cracking like fractured bone.
Before Amelia could blink:
GUNSHOTS.
Loud. Close. Real.
Bullets burst through the drywall, ripping into the couch cushions, tearing through picture frames. Amelia screamed, ducking low, her hands flying over her head. Zora dropped behind the coffee table like she'd done this before—like muscle memory.
The door swung fully open.
And three large men stepped inside.
Not nervous.
Not frantic.
Calm.
Like hunters entering familiar territory.
Their eyes scanned the room until the tallest one—broad shoulders, scar across his cheek—smirked.

"Well, well, well..." he growled.

"So this is where you been hidden', **Shayla**."

Shayla.

Not Zora.

Not Zara.

Shayla.

Amelia's blood ran cold.

Zora's eyes widened—pure, raw fear igniting in her pupils.

"Please," she whispered. "Not here. Not her."

The second man snorted, raising his gun lazily like it was an extension of his own arm.

"You didn't think we'd find you?" he hissed. "After everything you stole? After how you disappeared in the middle of the night?"

Zora shook her head violently.

"That's not what happened"

"Oh spare us," the third man laughed. "You stabbed our boss. Left him like trash. You think you can just run to Cali and change your name, and we forget?"

The accusation slapped Amelia across the face.

Their boss.

OUR boss.

The man they found dead.

Zora's story.

Her panic.

Her fear of true crime.

Her new identity.

It all collided into a single horrifying realization:

Zora had more secrets than she'd ever admitted.

And those secrets had come for blood.

The tall man stepped forward, tapping the gun against his palm.

"We gave you time. We gave you warnings. You didn't listen."

His gaze slid to Amelia

slowly,

intentionally,

like he was peeling back her soul.

"And who's this?" he sneered.

"Your little friend?"

Icy dread flooded Amelia's veins.
She took a step back, inching toward the kitchen,
hands shaking,
breath shallow,
mind racing.
The men turned their attention to Zora again, arguing, threatening,
circling like wolves.
Amelia's flame rose in her chest
not courage,
not bravery,
but survival.
She backed up farther
toward the back door,
toward escape,
toward air.
Her mind screamed one thing:
Run.
Run now.
RUN.
While the men taunted Zora, while Zora begged, while the room
spun with danger
Amelia moved quietly.
Soft as wind.
Quick as fire.
Her feet sliding across the floor in tiny steps.
Her hand closed around the back doorknob.
Her heart hammered so loudly she thought they'd hear it.
But before she could twist it
The tall man's voice cut through the room like a blade.
"Where the hell do you think you're going?"
Amelia froze.
The room caught fire.
And for the first time, she realized
Zora wasn't the only one running anymore.
Now Amelia was part of the story.
Part of the danger.
Part of the fire.

Fire, Fury & The Truth In Blood

Amelia froze with her hand on the doorknob.
The tall man's voice sliced through the room like a sharpened blade:
"Where the hell do you think *you're* going?"
Every muscle in her body locked.
Every heartbeat roared in her ears.
She could feel her flame trembling,
threatening to extinguish under fear.
Zora's eyes snapped to her, widening in horror.
"Amelia—don't," she mouthed.
But it was too late.
The men were already closing in.

Amelia's Escape Attempt

Survival roared through Amelia's chest.
Her fire didn't whisper this time—it screamed.
She twisted the doorknob fast,
jerking it open in one desperate, adrenaline-fueled motion.
Cold air hit her face like freedom.
She lunged.
Bolted.
But she made it only two steps out the door before
A hand like steel clamped onto her arm.
She cried out as she was yanked backward with brutal force,
her feet leaving the ground for a split second. She hit the floor hard, air
knocked out of her lungs.
"Nice try, sweetheart," the third man sneered.
"You think we're letting witnesses walk out?"
Amelia gasped for breath, her vision blurring, but her fire
that stubborn, defiant flame refused to die.
She kicked, clawed, twisted, fought, desperate to break free.
But he was too strong.

Zora's Fire Erupts

The moment Amelia hit the floor, something in Zora *snapped*.

A sound tore out of her—half scream, half roar—pure fire finally unleashing itself.

"Don't touch her!"

She lunged at the man gripping Amelia, tackling him from the side with a strength Amelia didn't even know she had. They crashed into the wall, knocking a picture frame to the floor.

The tall man surged forward to intervene, but Zora swung.

Her fist cracked across his jaw with a sound that echoed like a gunshot. He stumbled, shocked.

"You want ME?" she screamed.

"COME FOR ME!"

The men regrouped, surprised by Zora's fury

but no one was more shocked than Amelia.

Because this wasn't the fire she'd seen on stage.

This wasn't poetry.

This was survival incarnate.

A woman fighting like she had nothing left to lose.

She positioned herself between the men and Amelia

arms spread,

breathing heavy,

eyes burning like the center of a flame.

"You won't touch her," Zora hissed.

"You won't hurt another woman. Not again."

The Truth Detonates

The tallest man spat blood onto the floor, wiping his jaw.

"You really think you're some kind of hero, Shayla?"

Zora flinched at the name.

"You think you're protecting her?"

He laughed cruelly.

"You can't even protect yourself."

Zora didn't move.

Didn't blink.

Didn't breathe.

He smirked.

"How about we tell your little friend the real story? Since you're so interested in playing Saint Zora."

Amelia felt her stomach drop.

The men exchanged glances—then one stepped toward Amelia, bending down so he was eye-level, his breath hot and toxic.

"You think she ran because of some abusive boyfriend?"

He chuckled.

"Cute story."

Zora's body trembled with rage.

"Shut up," she snarled.

But the man ignored her.

"You want to know what happened to your boss?

The man you found dead on that office floor?"

Amelia's blood turned to ice.

"We didn't kill him," the man said.

"But Zora here?"

He tilted his head.

"She sure had motive."

Zora shook her head violently.

"No—no, Amelia, that's not"

The man cut her off.

"He blackmailed her."

His smile was venom.

"He found out who she really was.

About her 'ex.'

About her old life.

About what she did to get away."

Amelia's breath hitched.

"He threatened to turn her in unless she paid him. And when Zora didn't pay?"

He let the silence linger.

"He ended up dead."

Zora screamed,

"That's a LIE!"

Her voice cracked like burning wood.

"I didn't kill him! Amelia, I didn't! He hurt me, yes—he tried to force me—he threatened me but I DIDN'T kill him!"

The men laughed, cruel and dismissive.

"Sure. Keep telling her that."

The Room Catches Fire

The world around Amelia spun.
Truth, lies, fear, loyalty, fire
all crashing at once.
Her flame quivered painfully.
Who was telling the truth?
Were any of them?
Was everyone lying?
She pushed herself up slowly, chest heaving, tears burning her eyes—not from weakness, but from too much heat inside her body at once.
The tall man raised his gun again.
"We're done playing."
He aimed
not at Zora
but at Amelia.
Zora lunged forward.
"NO!"
And in that split second
a sound tore through the room.
A new sound.
A sharp, bright, violent sound.
Another gunshot.
But this one
this one didn't come from the men.
It came from the doorway behind them.
Someone else had arrived.
And the real story was about to explode.

The Shot That Changed Everything

The gunshot cracked through the room like lightning splitting a tree.
Everyone froze.
Everyone turned.
Smoke curled in the doorway.
And standing there, gun trembling in her hand, eyes wide with fear and fury, was a woman Amelia had never seen before.
But Zora had.

Her face drained of all color.
Her knees buckled.
Her breath caught in her throat.
"Mama...?"
Amelia's mind stuttered.
This woman didn't look like the mother Zora had described
the addict,
the ghost,
the woman lost to crack pipes and broken promises.
No.
This woman looked like fire in human form—
older, battered, but blazing.
Like someone who had crawled her way out of her own ashes.
Her voice shook with rage.
"Get the hell away from my daughter."

The Men React — And The Real Twist Unfolds

The three intruders staggered backward, surprise flashing across their faces.

"Vanessa?" the tallest one spat.

"You alive?"

The woman—Vanessa—cocked the gun again with shaking hands.

"I been alive," she hissed. "Just invisible. Y'all didn't think I'd let you take my baby again, did you?"

Again.

The word hit Amelia like a punch.

Zora's eyes filled with tears.

"Mama... what are you doing here?"

Vanessa didn't look at her.

Her eyes never left the men.

"You think I didn't know they'd come for you?" she snapped. "I've been watching. I been waiting. You think I survived the streets for nothing? I knew they'd track you."

Amelia's head spun.

Zora had told her her mother was an addict.

Broken.

Gone.

But this woman
this firestorm standing in the doorway
was anything but gone.
She was controlled flame.
Directed heat.
A mother who had done terrible things
but would not let harm touch her child again.
Vanessa's eyes darted to Amelia for one second.
"You the friend?" she barked.
Amelia swallowed. "Yes."
Vanessa nodded once.
"Then you need to move. Now."

Amelia's Discovery — The Truth Behind The Truth

While the men and Vanessa yelled, Amelia's gaze dropped to the floor...

...to the wallet one of the men had dropped in the chaos.
Curiosity—survival—her fire—pulled her toward it.
She crouched, snatched it up, and opened it quickly.
Her body went rigid.
Inside was a photo.
A photo of their boss.
But not in the office.
Not dead.
Alive.
Smiling.
Standing with
Amelia's breath collapsed.
Standing with Zora.
Arm around her.
Laughing.
Too close.
Too intimate.
On the back of the photo:
**"To my Shayla — partners forever.
No more running."**
Amelia's blood ran cold.

Partners?
Partners in WHAT?
Zora never mentioned partnership.
Only blackmail.
Only threats.
The fire inside Amelia twisted painfully.
What if the truth wasn't just dark
what if it was *different* than both stories she'd been told?
She looked up at Zora.
Still fighting.
Still protecting her.
Still burning.
She looked down at the photo again.
And her flame wavered.

The Fight Erupts — Fire On All Sides

The tallest man lunged toward Vanessa.
Zora screamed,
"NO!"
Amelia watched in horror as Vanessa fired again
the bullet grazed his arm, sending him stumbling into the wall.
The man with the scar charged at Zora.
She kicked him in the knee, elbowed him in the throat, fighting with
a ferocity Amelia had never seen.
"AMELIA!" Zora shouted.
"GO! NOW!"
Amelia hesitated photo clenched in her fist, secrets burning holes
in her palm.
"Go!" Vanessa yelled. "I'll hold them!"

The Escape — Two Flames Running Into The Night

Zora grabbed Amelia's wrist and yanked her toward the back door.
This time, they made it.
They burst into the alley, breathless, hearts hammering like drums.
Sirens blared somewhere in the distance.
Dogs barked.

Lights flickered.
Zora didn't let go of her hand.
"Run," she gasped.
"Don't look back."
And Amelia ran with her
air burning her lungs,
feet pounding pavement,
flame roaring in her chest.
But the whole time, the photo pressed against her palm
like a wound,
like a warning,
like a truth she couldn't un-see.
Zora stumbled beside her, terrified, shaking.
Amelia looked at her—
And for the first time since they met, she wasn't sure if she was running *with* fire or *from* it.

Truth Burns, But So Does Loyalty

They ran until their lungs were raw,
until their legs trembled,
until the night swallowed them whole.
Zora finally pulled Amelia into the shadows behind an abandoned laundromat.
Both of them gasped for air, sweat dripping down their temples, fear clinging to them like smoke.
But Amelia couldn't breathe.
Not from running, but from the photo burning in her fist.
Zora reached for her arm.
"You okay?"
Amelia jerked away.
"Don't," she said sharply.
Zora froze.
Amelia held up the photo the edges crumpled from her grip.
"Explain this," she whispered, voice trembling with confusion, fear, and betrayal.
Zora's eyes widened—
pain, panic, and recognition flickering across her face.

"Amelia... where did you..."

"It fell out of one of their wallets," Amelia said. "Tell me. Who is he to you? Because this"—she shook the picture—"this is not blackmail. This is not threats. This is not a man you were scared of."

Zora stepped back, her fire turning inward.

"Amelia, it's not what you think."

"Then tell me what it is."

Vanessa's Backstory
The Real Flame Behind The Fire

Before Zora could speak, footsteps pounded toward them.

Both women spun toward the sound, but it was Vanessa staggering into the alley, her gun tucked into her waistband, her breathing labored.

"Come on," she rasped. "We don't have time. They're regroupin'. We need to get in the car."

Zora rushed to her mother's side.

"Mama—are you hurt?"

"Nothin' I ain't used to," Vanessa snapped, brushing her off. Then she fixed her sharp gaze on Amelia—like she could see all the questions burning behind her eyes.

"You wanna know the truth?" Vanessa said. "Fine. I'll tell you."

She leaned against the brick wall, wincing.

"I've been tracking those men for weeks," she said. "They ain't just criminals—they're part of a crew your boss worked for."

Amelia blinked.

"Our boss... worked for *them*?"

Vanessa nodded grimly.

"He wasn't no victim. He was one of 'em."

Amelia's stomach twisted.

"You said Zora told you he was blackmailing her," Amelia whispered.

Zora looked away.

"He was," Vanessa said sharply. "But not for what she told you."

Amelia turned to Zora, heart crumbling.

"What. Did. He. Know?"

Zora closed her eyes, tears forming.

"I didn't tell you everything."

The Real Truth — Zora & The Boss

Zora took a shaky breath.

"I met him years ago," she said. "Back when I was still Shayla. Back when I was running with a bad crowd."

Amelia's heart sank.

"We weren't partners in crime," Zora said quickly. "Not like that. But we grew up in the same circles. Same streets. Same survival."

She swallowed hard.

"He wasn't evil at first. He was… like me. Hurt. Broken. Doing whatever he could to stay alive."

She looked at the picture, shame burning her cheeks.

"Yes, we were close once. Not lovers. Not romantic. But close enough that we trusted each other."

Vanessa cut in, voice low and bitter.

"Too much trust. He got tangled up with those men, and when he wanted out, they dragged Zora into it."

Zora nodded, wiping her tears.

"He told them I owed them. Said I needed to work with them. Run product. Help launder money. I told him no."

Amelia whispered, "And then?"

"He snapped," Zora said. "Said he'd expose everything about my past. Said he'd tell the cops what happened with my ex. Said I'd go down for something I didn't mean to do."

Zora's voice cracked.

"He wanted to own me. To control me. To make me scared."

Her body trembled.

"And then… the night he died…" she whispered, her voice faint.

"I didn't kill him, Amelia. I swear I didn't."

Vanessa stepped forward, pulling a folded paper from her pocket.

"And we got proof."

The Proof — A New Revelation

Vanessa handed Amelia the paper.

Amelia opened it with trembling fingers.

It was a **police report**.

About the boss.

About the night he died.
About a witness who saw "a tall man with a scar" leaving the scene.
The same man who broke into Amelia's house.
The same man who pointed a gun at her.
The same man Zora had fought.
"He killed him," Vanessa said. "Not Zora."
Amelia's knees weakened.
Zora whispered, "I didn't know he had proof, Mama..."
Vanessa softened for a second.
"That's because you ran before I could show you. I've been tryin' to find you for months, baby."
Amelia stared at the report, then at Zora, then at Vanessa.
The truth hurt.
The truth healed.
The truth burned—but it also illuminated.
Her flame steadied.
But before anyone could breathe
A shout tore through the alley.
"There they are!"

The Hunt — Men Swarm The City

Headlights flared at the alley entrance.
Four more men spilled out of two black SUVs.
Amelia gasped.
Zora grabbed her hand.
Vanessa raised her gun again, fire in her eyes.
"RUN!"
They sprinted into the night
dodging dumpsters,
vaulting fences,
their hearts pounding like war drums.
Shouts echoed behind them.
Footsteps thundered.
Engines revved.
The city became a maze of shadows and danger.
Amelia ran with everything she had.
But she wasn't running from Zora anymore.

Not from her fire.
Not from her past.
She was running with her.
Because the truth was finally clear:
Zora wasn't a monster.
She wasn't a murderer.
She wasn't a liar.
She was hunted.
And now,
so was Amelia.
Two flames
burning together
against the dark.

The Choice That Burns

They finally stopped running when their legs gave out.

Hidden behind an abandoned warehouse, breathless, shaking, covered in sweat and adrenaline, Zora leaned against a wall, chest heaving.

Amelia stepped away from her not far, but far enough that there was space between their flames.

Real space.

Heavy space.

The kind that's filled with too many truths.

Zora looked at her, eyes swollen, desperate, terrified.

"Amelia… please. Say something."

Amelia couldn't.

Her heart was a battlefield. Her mind a wildfire of fear, loyalty, doubt, and truth. Her flame—once so steady, so sure—now flickered violently in her chest.

She stared at Zora, at the woman she had admired, trusted, connected with.

A woman filled with brilliance, trauma, strength, and secrets.

A woman who had kept too much from her.

A woman whose past didn't just have shadows
it had bodies.

Violence.

Enemies.

Men willing to shoot through doors to find her.

And suddenly, the thought she had been avoiding slammed into her with brutal clarity:

What if I had let her meet my twins?

Her breath caught.

Her stomach twisted.

Her entire body tensed like a flame fighting wind.

Amelia's Inner Thoughts

Dear God...

What if this had happened with my babies in the house?

What if those men had come looking while my twins were inside?

What if bullets had ripped through the walls...

while my children slept behind them?

No.

No.

I can't risk that.

I can't risk them.

I was right.

I was right to keep her at a distance.

Right not to introduce them.

Right not to let their worlds collide.

My children are my fire.

My sacred flame.

And Zora's fire...

her fire is dangerous.

Not because she is evil

but because the world hunting her is.

And I can't let that world touch mine.

The Moment Of Choice

Zora stepped closer, voice breaking.

"Amelia... please. Don't give up on me. I told you the truth. I've only ever wanted to protect you."

Amelia shook her head violently.

"No. Zora, you didn't tell me the truth. Not all of it."

Zora's shoulders slumped.

"You kept pieces. Big pieces. Dangerous pieces," Amelia whispered.

"You brought me into something I didn't understand. You risked my life—without giving me the chance to say no."

Zora opened her mouth to speak, but Amelia cut her off.

"And the worst part?"

Her voice cracked.

"You wanted to meet my twins. You kept asking. And I kept saying no because something in me knew."

Hot tears slid down her cheeks.

"I *felt* the fire around you.

I felt the danger in your past.

Even when I didn't understand it."

She swallowed hard.

"And now?

Now I know I was right."

Zora looked like she had been stabbed.

Not physically, but in her soul.

"Amelia..." she whispered, voice trembling. "I would never—never—hurt your kids."

"I know," Amelia said through tears. "I know *you* wouldn't. But the people chasing you? The people from your past? They don't care who they hurt."

Silence fell a deep, heavy silence that tasted like grief.

Zora sank to her knees, hands covering her face.

"I'm so sorry," she sobbed. "I didn't want this for you. I didn't want any of this."

Amelia knelt with her

not touching her,

but beside her.

"I believe you," Amelia whispered. "But believing you doesn't make it safe."

Zora looked up, heartbroken.

"So what are you saying?" she asked, voice barely audible.

Amelia's flame steadied just enough for her to speak her truth.

"I'm saying I can't let you near my twins.

Not until your past stops hunting you.

Not until the fire around you stops setting everything on edge."

Zora's face crumpled.
"Does that mean... you're leaving me?"
Amelia closed her eyes.
"No," she whispered.
"I'm not leaving you."
She opened them again, tears blazing.
"But I'm stepping back.
Until I know what's real.
Until I know you're safe.
Until I know I can trust every part of your truth."
Zora swallowed a sob.
"And until then?" she choked.
Amelia looked her straight in the eyes.
"Until then...
I choose my children.
I choose safety.
I choose distance."
A single tear traced Zora's cheek.
"And... do you still choose me?" she whispered.
Amelia exhaled a trembling breath.
"I don't know yet," she said honestly.
"But I'm not abandoning you.
Fire doesn't abandon fire.
But it does protect what it loves."
Zora bowed her head.
And in that moment,
the two flames sat side by side in the dark
not extinguished,
not intertwined,
but burning separately,
trying to find a way back to each other
without burning everything else down.

When Fire Walks Away To Save What It Loves

Zora was gone by morning.
No goodbye.
No text.

No voicemail.
No explanation.
Just absence.
A silence so heavy it felt like ash in the air.
Amelia noticed it the moment she woke.
The apartment was too still, too empty, as if Zora's fire had been holding the walls up, and now everything leaned inward, sagging, grieving.
On the counter was a single note:
"Stay safe.
Stay away from me.
Z"
The handwriting trembled.
The ink was smudged—either from tears or from haste.
Amelia stared at it until her vision blurred.
Her chest tightened.
She whispered to herself, "Why would she leave like this… after everything?"
But deep down, she knew.
Zora was running again
not because she wanted to,
but because her past had walked too close.
And because Amelia had children.
Zora had seen the fear in her eyes last night.
She had seen the decision forming.
So she made it for her.
She walked away.

Zora's POV
The Fire That Burns Itself To Save Others

Zora didn't run gracefully.
She stumbled.
Her breath shook with every inhale.
Her ribs ached from where one of the men had hit her.
Her wrists were bruised.
Her palms bloodied from climbing fences in the dark.
But none of that hurt as much as leaving Amelia did.

"You deserve peace," Zora whispered into the empty dawn.
"Not flames that follow you home."
She ducked behind dumpsters, moved through alleys, avoided streets with cameras.
She'd been running since she was sixteen
but it had never felt like this.
This wasn't running for survival.
This was running from someone she cared about.
Someone who saw her fire and didn't flinch.
Someone she wanted to protect more than she wanted to breathe.
Zora wiped a tear with the back of her hand.
"Mama was right… everything I touch burns."
The gang had been closing in for weeks.
The scarred man was just the beginning.
More were coming.
More dangerous.
More desperate.
And Amelia—gentle, fierce, flame-hearted Amelia—was the only innocent in the line of fire.
So Zora did the only thing she knew how to do.
She disappeared.

Amelia
The Clues Left Behind

Amelia couldn't sit still.
Her chest hurt with a dull ache that spread like heat across her sternum. She had no appetite. Her hands shook as she tried to make coffee.
Everything inside her screamed that something was wrong.
So she went searching
through the apartment,
through the things Zora had left behind.
In Zora's room, she found:

- A prepaid phone snapped in half
- A duffel bag missing
- A burner notebook filled with coded addresses
- Newspaper clippings about the gang

- And one picture she hadn't seen before
  A photo of **Zora as a teenager**, bruised, holding a baby.
Amelia covered her mouth.
"Oh my God..."
She flipped the picture over.
On the back, in shaky handwriting:
"For protection."
Not for guilt.
Not for running.
Not for revenge.
For protection.
Amelia's heart twisted painfully.
Every day Zora had lived was a day she was trying to outrun someone else's violence.
And now that violence was circling again.

The Men Get Closer

It started with a van parked across the street.
Then another one.
Then two unfamiliar men walking past the house multiple times that day.
Then a third man who paused at Amelia's mailbox.
Amelia's skin prickled.
Her stomach dropped.
They weren't just looking for Zora.
They were mapping the area.
Looking for her.
Looking for witnesses.
Looking for leverage.
Looking for Amelia.
She locked every window.
Double-checked the doors.
Closed every curtain.
But she felt the danger like a second heartbeat.
Her flame rose, trembling and fierce.
"Zora... what did you get yourself into?"

The Plot Twist — Zora's Ex Returns

That night, a shadow moved across Amelia's porch.
A knock.
Not loud.
Not urgent.
Just… deliberate.
Amelia froze.
Her throat tightened.
She peeked through the blinds and her blood turned cold.
A tall man stood outside.
Scar across his cheek.
The same man from the alley.
But he wasn't alone.
Another man stepped into the porch light, a face Amelia had never seen before:
Sharp eyes.
Heavy jaw.
A tattoo of a crown at the base of his neck.
He looked up, directly at her hidden face behind the curtain—as if he could sense her watching.
He smiled.
And then he said

**"Tell Zora Shayla…
her ex sends his love."**

Amelia's heart sank.
Zora's ex wasn't dead.
He was alive.
Alive—and hunting.
And worse—
He was working with his brother.
The man with the crown tattoo tapped the door gently.
"Tell her she can't run forever."
Amelia backed away, pulse spiraling into panic.
"They're close," she whispered.
"Oh God—they're already here."

Amelia's Final Decision — Ending The Friendship

Amelia grabbed her phone with shaking hands.
She didn't know where Zora was.
She didn't know if the message would reach her.
She didn't even know if Zora was still alive.
But she knew she had to protect her children.
So she typed the hardest words she had ever written:
"Zora...
they came to my house.
They know where I live.
I can't do this anymore.
I can't risk my kids.
I'm sorry...
but our friendship has to end.
Please don't come back."
Her thumb hovered.
Her eyes filled.
Her fire cracked, dimmed, broke.
And she pressed **send**.
The message delivered instantly.
No typing bubbles.
No reply.
No goodbye.
Just more silence.
Amelia sank onto the couch, tears dripping onto her shaking hands.
She whispered into the emptiness:
"I'm sorry... I'm so sorry..."
Because she loved Zora.
As a friend.
As a sister in fire.
As someone who had cracked her open in ways she didn't expect.
But love wasn't enough.
Fire wasn't enough.
Not for this.
Her twins were the only flames she could protect.
And Zora's fire—uncontrolled, hunted, marked—could burn their
entire world to ash.
So Amelia ended the friendship.

To save her children.
To save herself.
And maybe, in the deepest part of Zora's heart, to save Zora too.

Zora had found temporary refuge in a forgotten, boarded-up apartment on the far edge of the city. The place smelled like mildew and old rain. The wallpaper hung from the walls like shedding skin. Every footstep stirred dust that danced in the slivers of moonlight cutting through cracked windows.

It wasn't shelter it was a graveyard wearing the shape of a room.

She sat on the floor with her back against splintered wood, her entire body aching.

Her ribs throbbed.

Her knuckles pulsed with heat.

Her legs quivered from running through alleyways
until her muscles screamed.

Her breath rattled like broken glass in her chest.

She felt like a fire someone had tried to beat out with their bare hands.

Then her phone vibrated.

A single buzz.

A single message.

A single moment that split her entire life in half.

She unlocked the screen, her fingers trembling so hard she could barely swipe. The message glowed in the darkness like a knife blade catching moonlight.

"Zora...

they came to my house.

They know where I live.

I can't do this anymore.

I can't risk my kids.

I'm sorry...

but our friendship has to end.

Please don't come back."

Zora didn't inhale.

She didn't exhale.

Her heart didn't merely crack—it **ruptured**, like a burning log collapsing under its own heat.

Her knees buckled, and she folded onto the dusty wooden floor, hands shaking uncontrollably.

The phone slipped from her grasp, clattering against the boards, the sound echoing through the empty room like a gunshot.

Her sobs tore out of her in choked, violent bursts—raw, ugly, uncontrollable. Tears streamed down her face so fast they dripped off her chin, darkening the floor beneath her like tiny, spilled storms.

"Amelia…" she gasped between sobs, clutching her stomach as if trying to hold herself together. "I never wanted to hurt you… I never wanted this…"

She felt her chest cave inward, the fire inside her shrinking to a faint, flickering ember.

For the first time since she was a child hiding under a table during one of her mother's withdrawals

Zora wanted her flame to go out.

The silence swallowed her.

She curled into herself, small and trembling, like a extinguished match tossed into darkness.

Zora's Ex
Making His Move

Across town, a flickering streetlamp buzzed above two men standing in the shadows. One of them—tall, lean, a scar slicing across his cheek like a lightning strike—looked bored. The other, Zora's ex, rolled a cigarette between his fingers, smirking as he stared at his phone screen.

The picture showed Zora and Amelia laughing in the sunlight. Two women unaware the world hunted them.

"So this is the bitch she protectin'," he murmured, tapping the screen with a slow, deliberate rhythm.

His brother chuckled darkly.

"They say she got kids."

Zora's ex's eyes gleamed with cruelty.

"Good.

Makes her easier to control."

He lit the cigarette, the flame briefly illuminating his face—a face shaped by violence, bruised ego, and obsession. The smoke curled around him like a lazy serpent.

"Shayla always cared too damn much… about everybody but me."
He dialed a number.
"Find her mother," he said, each word dripping venom.
"Bring her in."
Then he glanced at the picture again, his voice dropping to a chilling whisper:
"And when Shayla comes runnin'?
I'm gonna make her watch everything burn."

Amelia
A Terrifying Clue

Three days crawled by like shadows stretching across a floor.
Amelia moved through them like a ghost.
She took her twins to school.
She worked.
She cooked.
She washed dishes.
She locked every door twice.
She slept with a bat beside her bed.
She did everything *right*—
but the silence from Zora echoed behind every thought.
Then, on a windless afternoon, she opened her mailbox.
Bills.
Coupons.
A folded school newsletter.
And an unmarked envelope.
No name.
No stamp.
Just a weight that felt wrong.
Her hands trembled as she opened it.
Inside was a single glossy photograph.
Zora's duffel bag.
Ripped open.
Thrown into dirt.

Its contents spilled like organs.
And beside it
Zora's hoodie.
The one she wore the night she ran.
Stained with fresh, dark blood.
Amelia's breath caught in her throat.
"No..."
Her voice quivered, barely a whisper.
"No no no..."
The world tilted.
The sidewalk spun.
Her knees nearly buckled.
She pressed her back against the mailbox, sliding down until she was sitting on the ground.
She flipped the photo over with shaking fingers.
On the back, written in jagged letters:
"Come get your friend."
Amelia's heart shattered.
"Dear God...did they kill her?"
A cold wind swept across her face, raising goosebumps across her arms.
Her twins ran up behind her, laughing from school.
"Mom? You okay?"
Amelia snapped the picture behind her back.
"Yes," she lied, her voice thin. "Everything's fine."
But nothing was fine.
Nothing.
A small flame flickered painfully in her chest—a mix of guilt and dread.
"I walked away," she whispered.
"And something happened to her..."
She felt it deep, deep inside her bones.
This wasn't just a threat.
It was an invitation.
A trap.
A message written in blood.

Vanessa
The Dangerous Confrontation

Vanessa felt something was wrong before the men even appeared.
Call it intuition.
Call it old instincts.
Call it the ghost of the woman she used to be.
The night was too silent.
The air too still.
The shadows too thick.
She stepped outside her back door, gun raised. But, the moment her foot touched the porch, a shadow moved behind her.
Then another.
Then another.
Four men emerged, their faces half-hidden in darkness, their boots crunching on gravel.
"Evenin', Miss Vanessa," one of them sneered.
Vanessa didn't flinch.
"Where's my daughter?" she snapped, her voice low and steady.
The scarred man stepped closer, his smile slow and cruel.
"Alive.
For now."
She cocked her gun.
"You touch her..."
"You'll do what?" he mocked, taking another step.
"You forget who you used to run with?"
Vanessa's stomach dropped.
Another man laughed—a hollow, ugly sound.
"You helped us build this empire. You think you just get to walk away? Play mama? Pretend you changed?"
Vanessa raised her chin, fire flickering behind her eyes.
"Zora ain't part of this life no more."
The scarred man smirked.
"Yeah? Well in this life, we decide when you're done."
Before she could pull the trigger, one man lunged forward, grabbing her wrist and twisting it until her gun clattered onto the concrete.
Another drove a boot into her ribs.
Vanessa hit the ground, gasping.

She tried to claw her way up, but they swarmed her—boots, fists, hands gripping her hair.

"You gonna tell us where she is," one growled, pressing a gun to her head, "or we'll take our time with you."

Vanessa spit blood at his shoe.

"I ain't tellin' you shit."

He smiled.

"Good.

I was hopin' you'd say that."

Then the world went black.

Amelia
Stepping Out Of The Fire

Amelia sat alone at her kitchen table that night.

The lights dim.

The house quiet.

Her twins asleep upstairs.

Zora's bloodstained hoodie stared up at her from the photograph.

Every instinct in her body screamed to run to Zora, to find her, to help.

But her children's faces flashed in her mind.

This wasn't just Zora's fire anymore. It wasn't even hers. It was a wildfire that would swallow everything she loved.

She whispered into the empty kitchen: "It's not my fight anymore."

Her hands trembled as she picked up the picture.

"God protect her," she whispered, tears sliding silently down her face. "But don't let her bring this into my home."

She slid the photo into a drawer.

Closed it.

Locked it.

Turned off the light.

And walked away from the fire.

But somewhere deep inside her chest, in the place where her own flame lived, a small whisper burned:

This isn't over.

Fire always finds fire.

Generational Fire

We are women who survived **generational fire**,
not the kind that warms,
the kind that was meant to erase us.
We learned to cook from flames designed to consume us,
to season our pain with patience,
to stir resilience into every pot of memory.
What was supposed to burn us down
taught us how to feed nations.
We are women who danced barefoot across broken memories,
toes bleeding truth,
hips remembering joy before language did.
We learned rhythm from rupture,
balance from chaos,
grace from survival.
We are women who turned smoke into prayer
inhale grief,
exhale hope.
We learned how to speak to God through ash,
how to rise when visibility disappeared,
how to believe even when all we could see was gray.
And when she spoke
her voice cracked open the ceiling,
spilled truth across the room,
sent vibrations through bones that had been silent too long.
Every word carried history.
Every syllable lived.
This was not performance.
This was testimony.
This was fire remembering its purpose
not to destroy,
but to illuminate.
We are still here.
Still burning.
Still becoming.

What the Tail Knows

The tail is not the head.

It does not lead with voice or vision.

It follows.

And in survival, what follows often tells the truest story.

Amelia learned this early, long before she had words for it. Long before she understood trauma, or systems, or why some children were protected while others were returned to danger. Her body learned first.

The **tail** remembers what the mind tries to forget.

It holds the weight of what came before the drag of the past, the residue of fear, the ache that lingers even after the threat has passed. Like animals who survive by losing part of themselves to escape, Amelia learned that sometimes survival meant leaving pieces behind.

Not everyone survives whole.

Some survive by **shedding**.

The tail represents the part of Amelia that learned how to move after impact. How to keep going when the front of her life was forced to smile, perform, advocate, and lead while the back carried everything unspoken.

The tail is where reflex lives.

Where instinct curls.

Where balance is learned after collapse.

In Earth terms, the tail is the root that drags through soil. Bent. Scarred. Still functional.

Amelia's tail learned how to sense danger before it arrived. How to read rooms. How to stay quiet when noise meant punishment. How to follow rules that were never written but always enforced.

Her tail learned **adaptation**.

When the nightmare returned, it wasn't the past calling her back it was the tail asking to be acknowledged. Asking to be finished. Asking to stop dragging behind her, heavy and unnamed.

The tail becomes proof:

I survived the pull. I carried what I had to. I am still standing.

In Earth, the tail is no longer something to escape.

It is something to **stand upon**.

And when Amelia finally feels steady—when the ground no longer shifts beneath her feet—she realizes the truth:

What followed her did not define her future.

It supported it.

Grounding
When Amelia Meets Lauren

When Amelia met Lauren, it was in a waiting room that smelled faintly of burnt coffee and fresh hope. Two clipboards. Two pens. Two women pretending not to size up the room while quietly measuring their own readiness for whatever was next.

Lauren stood when her name was called—tall, brown-skinned, poised in a way that came from knowing herself. Her posture spoke before she ever did. She moved with intention, like someone who had learned how to stand firm without becoming rigid. A professional. A dynamic speaker. The kind of woman whose presence softened a room while sharpening its focus.

Amelia noticed.

Not out of comparison—but recognition.

There was something grounding about Lauren. Earth energy. Rooted. Stable. Like she had learned how to grow in places where the soil was not always kind.

They exchanged polite smiles at first. The kind you give strangers who feel oddly familiar.

Hours later, they found themselves sitting side by side again—this time not waiting but being welcomed. Both hired. Both selected. Both chosen to serve as community advocates.

It felt intentional.

As introductions circled the room, Amelia listened to Lauren speak. Her words were clear, confident, and compassionate. She spoke about community not as a buzzword, but as a responsibility. About advocacy not as a job, but as a calling. About people not as cases, but as stories still being written.

Amelia felt the ground beneath her steady.

After the meeting, conversation came easy. Not forced. Not surface-level. The kind that unfolds naturally when two people speak the same language of purpose.

They talked about the communities that raised them—and the ones that wounded them. About showing up even when tired. About holding space for others while learning, slowly, how to hold space for themselves.

Lauren listened deeply. Amelia spoke honestly.

There was no competition here. No posturing. Just mutual respect.

Earth meeting Earth.

Together, they understood the weight of the work. The emotional labor. The invisible load. The need for grounding rituals—breath, boundaries, reflection—so the work wouldn't consume the worker.

Lauren reminded Amelia that rest was not a reward, but a requirement. Amelia reminded Lauren that softness could still be strength.

They balanced each other.

In the days that followed, they walked neighborhoods together. Sat with families. Attended meetings that demanded patience and resilience. Some days were heavy. Others hopeful. All of them real.

And through it all, Amelia felt herself becoming more rooted.

Because Earth does that.

It teaches you how to stand.

How to stay.

How to grow without rushing.

When Amelia met Lauren, it wasn't just a meeting—it was a grounding. A reminder that healing happens in connection. That purpose deepens when shared. And that, sometimes, the soil knows exactly who to place beside you.

Both Amelia and Lauren were born and raised in Los Angeles, California—city soil that shaped resilience early. Concrete lessons. Sunlit hope mixed with survival. Their roots grew from the same ground, even if their paths had twisted differently to get there.

Over the years, their friendship deepened. Not loudly. Not dramatically. But steadily—like roots wrapping around one another beneath the surface. Amelia trusted Lauren in a way she hadn't trusted many people. Not because she told her everything—but because Lauren never demanded the truth before Amelia was ready to give it.

Amelia shared very little about her life. She had learned early that silence could be safer than honesty. That some truths, when spoken too soon, could reopen wounds instead of healing them.

But the body remembers what the mouth avoids.

The nightmares started coming back.

Not gentle dreams. Not vague memories. These were sharp. Vivid. Flashbacks that didn't ask permission. Her chest tightened. Her breath shortened. Panic arrived without warning sometimes in the middle of conversations, sometimes while walking familiar streets.

Lauren noticed.

She noticed the way Amelia's eyes would glaze over. The way her hands would tremble. The way her voice would disappear mid-sentence, as if she had stepped out of herself.

One afternoon, Lauren didn't push. She didn't pry. She simply grounded them both feet planted, voices low.

"You're not here right now," Lauren said softly. "But you can come back."

That was how the conversations started.

Slow. Careful. Anchored.

Amelia didn't tell everything at once. She couldn't. But pieces slipped out in fragments like soil loosening after years of drought. And Lauren listened without interruption, without shock, without judgment.

When Amelia finally spoke of the nightmares, Lauren didn't offer comfort wrapped in denial. She offered truth wrapped in strength.

"You can't outrun what still lives inside you," Lauren said. "You have to face it. Head on. Finish the nightmare."

Those words landed heavy but steady.

Earth words.

Amelia took the advice.

The nightmare always began the same way.

A day at the beach.

One of her mother's many male "friends" had taken Amelia and her older sister out. They called him Uncle James. The name felt safe then. Familiar. A lie disguised as family.

He drove as far as he could toward the water. No music. No warning. Just the sound of waves growing louder.

Then he put the car in neutral.

Stepped out.

And pushed.

Amelia remembered the scream of metal. The cold rush as water flooded the car. The weight of the ocean forcing its way in. The panic. The helplessness.

The water rose fast.

She remembered losing consciousness.

When Amelia awoke, there was a crowd around her. Hands pulling her from the water. Air burning her lungs back to life. Someone wrapped her in a blanket, rubbing warmth into her skin.

She turned her head to look for her sister.

She wasn't breathing.

Her skin was pale. Still. Gone.

The ambulance arrived. Time blurred. Sirens screamed what Amelia couldn't. They pronounced her sister dead at the scene.

Amelia was questioned.

And she told the truth.

The system did what it always did removed her and her remaining siblings from her mother's care. Again.

But safety was temporary.

They were later returned through family reunification. Another chance given. Another door opened back into danger. Another silent message sent to a child that survival was optional.

That her life was still negotiable.

Sitting with Lauren years later, Amelia finally let the story rest outside her body.

And for the first time, the nightmare didn't win.

Lauren didn't try to fix the past. She helped Amelia plant herself in the present. Helped her understand that surviving wasn't weakness it was evidence.

Earth doesn't erase what's buried.

It holds it.

Processes it.

Transforms it.

And Amelia rooted now in truth, in friendship, in grounding began to feel something new beneath her feet.

Stability.

Not because the past disappeared but because it no longer controlled where she stood.

Amelia had been missing the performing arts.

Not just the stage but the ritual of it. The breath before the mic. The way a room settles when truth is about to be spoken. The feeling of being seen without having to explain yourself.

So, when she decided to attend an open mic, it felt natural. Familiar. Necessary.

Amelia was used to traveling alone. Independence had long been her companion. She got dressed with intention comfortable, confident, grounded. Before leaving, she paused for just a moment at the door.

A strange feeling passed through her body. Not fear exactly more like awareness brushing against her spine.

She dismissed it.

Amelia always texted a friend the details of her outings. Where she was going. What time she'd arrive. What time she expected to leave. It wasn't paranoia it was practice. Survival habits refined into safety rituals.

She walked to her car.

As she pulled away, she noticed a man dressed in dark clothing. He stood near a vehicle she didn't recognize. Something about him made her slow her breath not in panic, but in attention. Amelia took a mental note of his face, his posture, the car he was driving.

The tail was working.

She arrived at the venue and chose valet parking close, visible, safe. The night was crowded. Voices layered over one another. Laughter spilled onto the sidewalk. Inside, energy buzzed with anticipation.

The open mic list was already full.

Amelia didn't feel disappointed. Instead, curiosity replaced it. She scanned the sign-up sheet and noticed a few names she recognized artists who didn't just perform, but *arrived* on stage. Then she read the fine print.

It was also poetry slam night.

Winner takes **$5,000 cash**.

Her lips curved into a small smile.

This should be interesting.

People mingled some rehearsing under their breath, others feeding nerves with jokes and drinks. Amelia found a spot where she could see the room clearly. Walls, exits, faces. Old habits but not anxious ones. Grounded ones.

The host stepped up to the mic.

They welcomed the crowd, went over the rules for the open mic list, then explained the slam portion of the night judges, time limits, no props, no music. Raw words only.

The lights dimmed.

Chatter softened into a hush.

That moment right before the first poet takes the stage always felt sacred to Amelia. Like the earth itself was holding its breath. Waiting.

She felt it in her feet.

In her spine.

In the tail.

This was the place where stories shed their silence. Where survival learned how to speak without apology.

Amelia wasn't performing tonight.

But she was present.

And sometimes, presence is the ground that everything else grows from.

As the first poet took the stage, Amelia felt it again.

That pull.

Not fear, recognition.

Her body shifted before her thoughts did. A subtle adjustment. Weight moving to the balls of her feet. Eyes scanning without panic. The tail doesn't scream. It alerts.

She glanced toward the side of the room and froze for half a breath.

The man.

Dark clothing. Same posture. Same stillness.

He stood near the back, half-shadowed, not engaging, not clapping. Watching. Not the stage *her*. His gaze wasn't curious. It was anchored. Familiar in a way that made Amelia's stomach tighten.

The tail stirred.

You noticed him before for a reason.

Her mind tried to rationalize it. Crowded places recycle faces. Coincidences happen. But her body didn't argue. It remembered what her mind had once been forced to forget that danger doesn't always announce itself loudly.

Sometimes it follows.

Amelia casually shifted her position, angling herself toward a group of people. She checked her phone without making it obvious. Sent a quick text to the same friend she always did.

At a poetry spot. Slam night. Valet parking. Will update soon.

She didn't look back right away.

Earth teaches patience.

When she did glance again, the man had moved closer. Not fast. Not obvious. Just closer than before. Close enough that she could feel the pressure of his presence without him touching her.

Her breath slowed.

The tail grounded her.

She reminded herself where she was. Lights. People. Sound. Exits.

She named them silently one by one anchoring herself in the present. This was not the ocean. This was not a car filling with water. This was now.

But instinct doesn't confuse time.

It connects patterns.

The man's eyes met hers briefly. Just long enough. No smile. No threat spoken. Then he looked away as if nothing had happened.

That was worse.

Amelia felt the shift deep in her spine the same place her body had learned to survive before her voice had learned to speak. The tail wasn't pulling her backward tonight.

It was guiding her forward.

She stood and moved deliberately not rushing, not reacting. She repositioned herself closer to the bar, closer to the host's sightline, closer to light. She spoke briefly to a woman beside her, creating a visible connection.

The man didn't follow immediately.

He waited.

Predators often do.

When Amelia stepped toward the restroom hallway, she felt him move again. The distance shortened too quickly this time. Her chest tightened but she stayed grounded.

She turned.

Not sharply. Not afraid.

Just enough to let him know

I see you.

Their eyes met again.

And this time, Amelia trusted what her tail already knew.

She didn't confront him. She didn't freeze. She didn't disappear into politeness.

She walked straight to staff.

Spoke calmly. Clearly.

"There's someone making me uncomfortable. I need assistance."

Earth doesn't explain itself.

It protects.

Staff responded immediately. Lights shifted. Eyes watched. The man noticed the attention and just as quietly as he had appeared, he retreated. Melted back into the crowd. Then out the door.

Gone.

Amelia stood still for a moment after.

Heart steadying. Feet firm on the floor.

She realized something important then not with fear, but with clarity:

The nightmare didn't own her instincts anymore.

The past didn't get to override the present.

Her tail had done what it was meant to do.

Not drag her back.

But keep her alive.

And as the next poet took the stage voice shaking, truth rising Amelia felt something new settle into her bones.

Trust.

Not in the world.

But in herself.

Murder at an Open Mic

The night was going well.

The poets were on fire.

The mic was hot truth after truth, voices landing where they were meant to land. The room felt alive, electric, like language was doing what it was born to do.

Amelia went back to her seat to enjoy the show.

She settled in, letting the rhythm return to her body. This was her medicine. This was the place where pain learned how to breathe without suffocating her. One poet after another delivered heat raw, honest, unforgettable. For a moment, everything felt aligned.

Then the energy shifted.

The list had been open, too open. Anybody could sign up. One performer got on the mic and dragged the night into something heavy and endless politics, socialism, racism no rhythm, no poetry, no breath. Just noise disguised as purpose. The fire cooled. The room grew restless. People started checking their phones. Chairs scraped. A slow leak of bodies headed outside.

Amelia stepped out too.

The space outside felt strange too quiet. Empty in a way that didn't match the crowd inside. A few people stood gathered in a corner, whispering, tense. Something in her chest tightened. Before she could name it, the door flew open and people poured back in, faces tight, eyes wide.

Concern moved faster than words.

Then the sound.

Gunshots.

Sharp. Loud. Everywhere.

Screaming followed. Someone went down. Bodies collided. People tripped over each other trying to run, trying to hide, trying to survive. The room that had just held poetry was now chaos chairs knocked over, drinks shattered, fear filling every space words once lived.

The police were called. Sirens replaced verses. An investigation started immediately.

No one knew who the woman was who screamed but everyone remembered the scream.

It cut through everything.

The man who had been on the mic was familiar. He frequented the space sometimes. He was known. But he had never been that radical before. Never that angry. Never that unchecked.

Someone said it out loud almost like a confession, almost like an accusation:

"I'm tired of our voices and our craft being saturated. Everybody is not a poet. Everybody should not take that title."

That's what the woman yelled.

Even now, people argue about what it meant.

The murder remains unsolved.

We were all there.

But no one saw anything.

People had been standing around. Watching. Listening. Breathing the same air. And still nothing. Or at least, that's what they said.

But someone knew something.

They always do.

So the community did what it always does when the system stalls it started its own investigation. Street directive. Quiet conversations. Patterns traced backward. Who left early. Who stayed silent. Who changed their story.

Poetry spaces are supposed to be sacred.

But that night proved something else too:

When truth is mishandled,
when platforms aren't protected,
when voices are loud but not accountable
art can turn into a weapon.
And the mic remembers everything.
Even when people pretend they don't.

The next day, the detective sat across from Amelia with a legal pad and tired eyes. The room was plain. Neutral. Designed to hold facts, not feelings.

But Amelia's body didn't enter the room neutrally.

Her **tail** was already awake.

As questions rolled forward *Where were you standing? Who did you notice? Did anything feel off?*—Amelia felt something shift beneath the calm she had practiced overnight. Not panic. Not fear.

Memory.

Not the kind that comes crashing in but the kind that rises from the ground when you stop running from it.

"I remembered something," she said.

The detective looked up.

Amelia closed her eyes briefly not to escape, but to ground. She felt her feet on the floor. Her spine straight. The drag of the past lining itself into clarity.

"The man," she said. "The one I noticed before the shooting. I saw him earlier that night. Before I even got to the venue."

She described him carefully. Dark clothing. His posture. The way he watched without moving. Not curious—calculating. She described the car too. The make. The color. A dent near the rear bumper. Something about the way it idled too long.

Then she said the thing that surprised even herself.

"I remember part of the license plate."

The detective's pen paused.

Amelia gave the number slowly. Confidently. It wasn't guesswork. It was instinct that had been collecting data long before her mind labeled it as important.

This was **TAIL (Earth)** at work.

The tail doesn't forget what the eyes catalog for survival.

It doesn't need permission to remember.

It stores what might matter later.

Amelia hadn't chased danger that night but she hadn't ignored it either. Her body had done what it learned to do long ago: observe, adapt, survive.

The detective thanked her. Said it mattered. Said it could help.

And for the first time, Amelia believed him.

Because this time, she wasn't a child being questioned after tragedy. She was an adult finishing a pattern.

Outside of official channels, the community was already moving.

Quietly.

Poetry communities talk. Not loudly but thoroughly. People compared notes without calling it that. Someone remembered the man leaving early. Someone else remembered seeing a similar car parked too close to the corner that night. Another person mentioned how the same man had been agitated before had spoken about voices being stolen, spaces being diluted.

Pieces began to align.

Not accusations patterns.

This wasn't vigilante justice. It was **street directive**—the same way communities have always protected themselves when systems lag behind lived experience. People checked in on each other. Shared what they noticed. Replayed the night from different angles.

Someone said, "He wasn't there for poetry."

Someone else said, "He was watching the room, not the mic."

Amelia listened more than she spoke.

Earth teaches patience.

She realized then that her survival had never been accidental not as a child, not as an artist, not as a witness. Her tail had been guiding her all along, helping her move through danger without becoming it.

This time, the nightmare didn't end in silence.

It ended in contribution.

Her instinct didn't just save her it gave something back to the truth.

And as the investigation deepened official and unofficial Amelia stood grounded in what she now knew:

Survival isn't just about getting out alive. Sometimes it's about remembering enough to change what happens next.

The tail had followed her this far.

Now it stood behind her steady, strong, and no longer dragging the past.

Holding her upright.
Holding the ground.

After the night of the shooting, the poet's name was spoken softly at first.

Candles appeared on the sidewalk outside the venue. Flowers leaned against brick walls. Handwritten notes said things like *gone too soon* and *say their names*, even when no one was quite sure which names belonged where.

The poet who was murdered had a family. That part everyone agreed on.

A mother who collapsed when the news came. A sister who kept replaying old videos, searching for answers in familiar laughter. A child who would grow up with stories instead of memories.

There were others too the injured.

Some shot.

Some trampled.

Some carrying wounds that didn't bleed but never stopped hurting.

The community showed up.

A visual was organized poets, artists, organizers, community leaders standing shoulder to shoulder. Candles lit. Mics opened. Tears shared. People spoke about safety. About sacred spaces. About how poetry should never cost you your life.

Local news stations came.

Cameras rolled.

Soundbites were clipped.

The story ran for a few weeks.

Then it faded.

Another headline replaced it.

Another tragedy took its place.

But the community didn't move on.

They couldn't.

People kept asking questions quietly now.

Not just *who did this*, but *why.*

They spoke about the poet's family. About the woman who was shot an innocent bystander, just there to listen, just there to feel something real.

They said the same things people always say when grief has no direction:

"They were good people."
"They didn't deserve this."
"This shouldn't have happened."
And yet
no one really knew them.
Not beyond the surface.
Not beyond the night.
The words *victim* were used generously. Comfortably. Like a blanket pulled over confusion.
Until the investigation closed.
The detective's statement landed heavier than any poem ever had.
The individuals harmed at the poetry event—the poet included—were part of a trafficking crew. Transporting people across state lines.
The room went silent when that truth surfaced.
The shooter was not random.
He was a father.
A father whose child had been taken.
Moved.
Sold.
Lost in the same network that had been hiding in plain sight
under the cover of art,
under the safety of community spaces,
under the assumption that familiar faces mean harmless intentions.
The shooter didn't come for poetry.
He came for answers the system never gave him.
The revelation cracked the community wide open.
Shock.
Anger.
Denial.
People argued.
People cried.
People didn't know where to place their grief anymore.
Were they still victims if they caused harm first?
Could a poet still be innocent if his work hid something monstrous? What about the woman who was shot who truly *was* innocent? What about the families who loved people they never fully knew?
There were no clean answers.
Just heavy ones.

The community had to sit with the discomfort of it all that sometimes harm wears a familiar face, that not every story is what it seems, that justice and vengeance are not twins, and that grief doesn't disappear just because the truth is complicated.

The candles eventually burned out.

The news vans moved on.

But the questions stayed.

And the poetry space?

It was never the same.

Because now everyone understood:

Being present doesn't mean being aware.

Being talented doesn't mean being truthful.

And not everyone who is harmed is innocent. But harm still ripples outward, touching lives that never asked to be part of the story.

The mic remembered.

So did the floor.

And the community forever changed. Learned that sometimes the hardest truth is realizing the line between victim and villain is not always where we want it to be.

The man in the dark clothing resurfaced after the investigation closed.

Not immediately.

Not loudly.

His name never made the news.

But his presence returned in fragments security footage reviewed again, tips that arrived too late to matter, whispers that finally had a shape now that the truth had been spoken out loud.

Amelia learned that he had been there for weeks before the shooting.

Different nights.

Different events.

Always watching.

Rarely speaking.

He never signed up for the mic.

He stood in the shadows of rooms meant for expression, studying exits, faces, rhythms. He blended in the way men do when they understand crowds better than people understand danger.

He wasn't part of the trafficking crew.

He wasn't family.

He was something else.

A runner.

A watcher.

Someone whose job was to make sure no one followed too closely, asked too many questions, or noticed patterns forming where silence was expected.

The car Amelia remembered the one that idled too long was registered under a shell company. Temporary plates. Paper trails designed to dissolve under pressure. The partial license plate she gave detectives didn't lead to an arrest, but it led to movement.

Enough movement to confirm what the community had already begun to sense:

This wasn't isolated.

The poetry space hadn't been targeted randomly. It had been used because art spaces feel safe, because trust lives there, because people don't suspect harm where vulnerability is encouraged.

The man in dark clothing had been doing what tails do best—following.

But not for protection.

For control.

Amelia realized something that unsettled her more than fear ever had: she hadn't been followed because she was careless. She had been noticed because she was aware. Because awareness disrupts operations that depend on invisibility.

The night she saw him watching her, something shifted.

He noticed that she noticed.

And that was enough to change the trajectory.

After the shooting, he disappeared completely. No more sightings. No more half-shadowed figures near venues. No quiet presence lingering too long by doors.

That kind of disappearance doesn't happen by accident.

It happens when exposure becomes a risk.

The community kept talking. Quietly now. Intentionally. New protocols formed without official names check-ins, buddy systems, watching the watchers. Art didn't stop, but innocence did.

Amelia carried the knowledge differently.

Not as paranoia.

As grounding.

TAIL (Earth) had done its work again not dragging her into danger, not forcing her into heroics but anchoring her in discernment. Teaching her that survival isn't always about escape. Sometimes it's about interruption.

The man in dark clothing followed stories.

Amelia followed instincts.

Only one of them was meant to last.

And when she returned to open mics months later different venue, different night she stood closer to the light, closer to people, closer to exits. She still trusted the art. She just no longer trusted the silence around it.

Because Earth remembers patterns.

And the tail doesn't forget who was watching.

Not anymore.

The investigation into the disappearance of **Zora Mayfield** began quietly.

There was no press conference. No missing-person flyers taped to poles. No urgency that matched who she was or how loudly she had lived.

Fire rarely receives the response it deserves.

Zora's name surfaced again only after the murder at the open mic when detectives started tracing timelines backward instead of forward. They weren't looking for poetry. They were looking for patterns. Places. Faces that appeared more than once in rooms that should have been safe.

Zora's last confirmed sighting was at a poetry venue.

So was the shooting.

Different nights.

Same kind of room.

Same kind of crowd.

Art spaces. Open mics. Slam nights where voices were encouraged, where vulnerability passed for safety, where people assumed familiarity meant protection.

Detectives began to connect what the community had already been whispering about.

Zora had been asking questions before she disappeared.

Not abstract ones.

Not metaphorical ones.

Questions about missing people. About movement across state

lines. About how certain faces kept showing up in spaces meant for expression, not surveillance. She had been naming things out loud that others preferred to code into poems.

Fire does that.

It illuminates what was meant to stay hidden.

The murder at the open mic shifted the lens. What had been treated as an isolated act of violence was now part of a longer thread one that included Zora's absence, the trafficking investigation that followed, and the realization that the venue had been more than a stage.

It had been a meeting point.

As detectives revisited witness statements from the night of the shooting, one detail resurfaced repeatedly—often dismissed at first, then noted, then circled in red.

A man in dark clothing.

Seen watching.

Seen lingering.

Seen before the shots and absent after.

Amelia had noticed him first.

Not because she was looking for danger but because her body had learned how to recognize it long before her mind tried to rationalize it away. Her statement became the connective tissue between Fire and Earth—between Zora's disappearance and the night poetry turned lethal.

Zora Mayfield hadn't vanished without reason.

And the murder at the open mic wasn't random.

Fire had exposed something.

Earth had remembered it.

Now the investigation was no longer just about who pulled the trigger but about who had been watching long before anyone fell.

Amelia knew the truth.

And because she knew it, she stayed quiet.

Zora Mayfield wasn't the person the community had turned her into after she disappeared. She wasn't just Fire in human form, brave and untouchable, burning for justice without consequence. That version was easier to mourn. Easier to defend.

But it wasn't the whole truth.

Amelia had seen the cracks long before the investigation named them. She had noticed the way Zora moved through rooms confident, yes, but also guarded. The way certain people lingered too close after shows. The way conversations stopped when Amelia approached. The way Zora sometimes spoke like someone trying to outrun something already gaining ground.

Zora hadn't just been asking questions.

She had been involved.

Connected to people who didn't belong in poetry spaces. People who didn't care about art, or justice, or community only leverage, transport, silence. Dangerous individuals who understood how to use proximity to culture as cover.

Amelia knew because they had come to her.

Not loudly.

Not directly.

Threats rarely arrive screaming.

They came wrapped in warnings.

In suggestions.

In "concern."

A car slowing too long near her home.

A message passed through someone she barely knew.

A name mentioned casually that wasn't meant to be casual at all.

Her family's names.

That was enough.

Earth teaches you when to stand firm and when to step back. Survival isn't always confrontation. Sometimes it's containment.

Amelia didn't speak Zora's name after that. Not publicly. Not privately. Not even in spaces where people were rewriting Zora into a hero because it helped them sleep at night.

She avoided the conversations. Changed the subject. Left rooms early when Zora came up. Let people assume her silence meant grief, confusion, or distance.

She let them be wrong.

Because Amelia understood something the community was still wrestling with:

Not everyone who exposes fire is clean of smoke.

And not everyone who disappears is innocent.

That didn't mean Zora deserved what happened to her. It didn't mean the violence was justified.

It meant the truth was layered and layers can be dangerous to peel back without protection.

When detectives circled back, Amelia gave them facts. Only facts. What she had seen. What she remembered. Never speculation. Never motive. Never names that would bring heat back to her door.

She had learned that lesson early in life.

Finish the nightmare but don't invite a new one.

So Amelia stayed grounded. Watched. Listened. Protected her family. Trusted her instincts the way she always had quietly, completely.

Fire had burned too close.

Earth had absorbed the damage.

And Amelia standing between what was known and what was never meant to be said chose survival over spectacle.

Because sometimes the bravest thing you can do is live long enough to tell the story later.

When it's safe.

Amelia knew the rules. The kind you learn without being taught. The kind that keep you alive. You don't talk to the police not because you're hiding guilt, but because they don't come for truth, they come for narratives. They put you in a trick bag, twist your words, drag your name when your story doesn't line up with what they already decided to hear. Shady questions. Shadier paperwork. Trust is a luxury you don't get when survival is on the line.

In Los Angeles, we learned early how to protect our own. Before hashtags. Before task forces. Before press conferences. We policed our streets because we had to. Neighborhood watch wasn't a program it was instinct. Elders on porches. Store owners who knew every face. Kids who grew up reading the air before crossing the block. Everybody watching out, not to control but to keep harm from spreading.

Someone always sees what's going on in LA streets. Always. Maybe not the cameras. Maybe not the reports. But the city knows itself. Word travels faster than sirens. Patterns get noticed. Warnings get passed quietly, hand to hand, look to look. Amelia trusted that system more than any badge because it had history, memory, and accountability. Because it wasn't perfect, but it was ours.

The Case of the Poet at the Open Mic (Cold Case)

They call it a cold case now.

Not because it stopped hurting

but because the system stopped touching it.

The file is thick. Witness statements stacked on top of one another like unfinished sentences. Photos of a venue that once held applause, now frozen in forensic stillness. Timelines that almost line up. Leads that led nowhere or somewhere people didn't want to follow.

The poet's name is still written in ink.

But the case?

Pencil.

Officially, the investigation stalled after the larger truth surfaced trafficking, retaliation, family revenge disguised as random violence. The shooter identified. The motive partially explained. Enough answers to close a chapter without ever finishing the book.

What remains unanswered is everything that happened *before* the mic went hot.

Who knew what.

Who watched who.

Who brought danger into a space built for release.

The community remembers the poet differently than the file does.

In the file, he is a victim of circumstance.

In the streets, he is a question mark.

People speak carefully now. Names softened. Stories trimmed. The language of grief mixed with the language of survival. Candles burned out, but conversations didn't. They just moved off record.

Cold cases don't go quiet.

They go underground.

Every few months, someone brings it up again at another open mic, another gathering, another vigil for someone else. "Remember that night?" they say. And everybody nods. Because everyone remembers exactly where they were standing when poetry turned into panic.

The venue changed protocols.

The community changed habits.

Artists started checking exits before checking sound levels.

And Amelia?

Amelia filed the night away where she keeps truths that can't be spoken freely yet. She knows the case isn't cold it's **contained**. Waiting.

Like embers under ash. Like Fire that hasn't found oxygen again.

Cold cases don't mean unsolved forever.

They mean the city is still deciding who is safe enough to tell the rest of the story.

Until then, the poet at the open mic exists in two places at once: a name in a file, and a presence that lingers every time someone steps to the mic and clears their throat.

The case is cold.

But the memory?

Still warm.

They say they have the shooter.

That's the part that confuses people the most.

A name exists.

A motive makes sense on paper.

A story fits just enough to satisfy headlines.

But belief is not evidence.

And belief doesn't hold up in court.

The case is considered cold because nothing that matters can be proven. No weapon recovered that can be conclusively tied to him. No fingerprints that survive scrutiny. No DNA that places him inside the venue at the exact moment the shots were fired. Surveillance footage that skips, blurs, or points just shy of certainty. Angles that miss the most important seconds.

And witnesses?

That's where the case truly freezes.

There are none willing to testify.

Not because people didn't see anything but because what they saw lives in a gray space where fear, loyalty, and survival intersect. Statements changed. Timelines softened. Memories suddenly became unsure. People who were clear that night became cautious the next morning.

Liability is a heavy word in communities that already carry enough weight.

Some witnesses disappeared from follow-ups. Others remembered just enough to say they were present but not enough to point. And those who knew more understood what speaking would cost them. Families. Safety. Stability. Silence became a form of protection.

The detectives knew it too.

Without cooperative witnesses, the case couldn't move forward. Circumstantial evidence only stretches so far before it snaps under cross-examination. Prosecutors won't take a case to trial unless they're sure it will hold and this one wouldn't.

Too many gaps

Too many risks.

Too much that could be turned back on the people already harmed.

So the file was marked inactive.

Not closed.

Not solved.

Cold.

A case doesn't have to be forgotten to be frozen. Sometimes it's preserved exactly where it is because moving it would expose too many truths at once.

The community understands that part, even if they don't say it out loud.

They know justice doesn't always arrive in courtrooms. Sometimes it lives in memory. In caution. In changed behavior. In the way people watch doors now. In the way mics are protected. In the way silence becomes strategy.

The shooter may be known.

But knowing isn't enough.

Not when fear outpaces proof.

Not when truth has too many witnesses and nonwilling to stand.

That's why the case remains cold.

Not because the fire went out

but because no one wants to be the next spark.

•••

The venue reopened.

No ceremony.

No long statement.

Just a new flyer, a fresh coat of paint, and a post that said

We're back.

People went on with their normal lives the way cities always do by stepping over what hasn't been resolved and calling it resilience. The chairs were put back. The mic was tested. Drinks were poured. Laughter returned, thinner at first, then louder, as if volume could erase memory.

Then the announcement dropped.

The slam prize had tripled.

First place: $15,000.

Second place: $10,000.

Third place: $5,000.

The money hit the community like a slap and a seduction at the same time.

Some people called it growth.

Others called it blood money.

"How do you raise the stakes in a room where someone lost their life?"

"Who benefits when the prize gets bigger but the truth stays buried?"

"Are we honoring art or baiting desperation?"

The uproar spread quickly. Group chats lit up. Side conversations grew sharp. Elders shook their heads. Young poets argued that opportunity doesn't wait for healing. That survival costs money too. That art deserves investment.

And maybe it did.

But something about the timing felt off.

Amelia watched it all from a distance. She read the posts without commenting. Let the arguments pass without adding her voice. She felt the familiar pull the stage calling her back, the mic whispering *you belong here.*

But the tail stirred.

Money changes rooms.

It changes intentions.

It attracts people who don't care about craft, only outcomes.

Amelia thought about the night the room went quiet for all the wrong reasons. About Fire silenced. About Earth absorbing what no one wanted to clean up. About how quickly grief had been replaced with incentive.

Amelia moved on.

Not in the way people expect no dramatic closure, no public declaration of healing. She simply kept living. Kept choosing moments of softness where she could. Every once in a while, she took herself out on a date. No agenda. No rush. Just good food, a quiet table, and permission to exist without being on guard.

That night, she was out to dinner alone when she met Wyatt.

It wasn't forced. No sparks flying across the room. Just an easy conversation that started with a comment about the menu and unfolded into something slower, steadier. They talked for hours about life, work, the city, the strange ways people find themselves exactly where they're meant to be. He listened without interrupting. Asked thoughtful questions. Didn't perform.

That mattered.

Amelia noticed how grounded he felt. Not flashy. Not trying to impress. His presence didn't demand anything from her. It felt anchored, like someone who knew who he was and wasn't trying to borrow identity from anyone else.

The conversation stayed calm.

That was how she knew.

She didn't imagine romance. She didn't rush meaning onto the moment. Amelia had learned the value of intention how important it was to let things build without pressure, without expectation.

A solid friendship felt right.

Something honest.

Something paced.

Something rooted in mutual respect.

They exchanged numbers without ceremony. No promises. Just a quiet understanding that connection doesn't have to be loud to be real.

As Amelia drove home later that night, she felt something unfamiliar but welcome settle into her chest not excitement, not fear.

Balance.

She smiled to herself, hands steady on the wheel.

Sometimes moving on doesn't mean leaving the past behind.

It means choosing who gets access to the present.

She wondered what kind of energy $15,000 would draw.

Who would show up hungry?

Who would show up watching?

She stood in front of her mirror, outfit half-chosen, phone in her hand, thumb hovering over the message she always sent when she went out.

Poetry spot. Slam night. Will update.

She hadn't decided yet.

Because attending meant presence.

And presence meant risk.

But absence meant surrendering space to people who didn't remember or didn't care to.

Amelia closed her eyes and listened not to fear, but to instinct.

And tried not to rush her decisions.

It waits for the ground to speak.

And the ground was saying:

Choose carefully.

Not whether to go.

But **why**.

The Night Amelia Returned to the Mic

Amelia decided not to go alone.

This time, she invited Laura and Wyatt to meet her at the poetry slam. Not for protection she was past that but for grounding. Laura came with her familiar steadiness, the kind that had carried Amelia through heavier seasons. Wyatt came with quiet curiosity, no expectations, just presence.

They both showed up.

That mattered more than they knew.

The venue felt different than Amelia remembered. Louder. Brighter. Hungrier. The prize money had changed the air $15,000 for first place but she didn't come for that. She came because something in her had settled enough to speak again.

When her name was called for the slam, she almost laughed.

What am I doing?

But her feet moved anyway.

The mic felt warm in her hands. Familiar. Like an old language returning to her tongue. She didn't think about judges. Didn't think about money. She spoke from the place that had survived everything the tail, the ground, the truth that doesn't ask permission.

The room went quiet.

Then alive.

When the scores were tallied, time stretched thin. Applause erupted before the announcement even finished.

"First place Amelia."

For a moment, she didn't move. The words didn't register. Laura was already on her feet, clapping, eyes bright. Wyatt smiled not surprised, just proud, like he had known this outcome belonged to her before she did.

The room rose.

A standing ovation.

Amelia looked out at the crowd, breath caught in her chest, disbelief blooming into gratitude. She had won. She really had. Not just the slam but the moment. The fear. The silence that once tried to keep her seated.

And then

She saw her.

Zora.

Standing near the back, half-lit, unmistakable. Fire where fire had always been. Watching, not smiling, not clapping just *present*. For a split second, Amelia's heart skipped. The room seemed to tilt.

She blinked.

The space shifted. The back of the room filled with movement again people cheering, phones raised, voices calling her name.

Zora was gone.

Amelia exhaled slowly and shook it off.

She accepted the check with steady hands. Hugged Laura. Thanked Wyatt. Let the moment be what it was earned, real, rooted. Whatever she had seen, she didn't chase it.

Some truths visit to remind you of how far you've come.

Some fires burn only long enough to light the way.

That night, Amelia walked off the stage grounded, carrying victory, community, and the quiet knowing that she was exactly where she was meant to be.

First Round Poem — "Still Standing" (Call-and-Response)

I come from a place
where silence was survival
and survival was mistaken for weakness.
(*Pause*)
If you've ever had to stay quiet to stay alive
say "I know."
Crowd: *I know.*

I learned early
how to read rooms
before I learned how to read books.
How to watch hands.
Watch exits.
Watch people who smile too hard
and listen too little.
If you learned safety before you learned comfort
say "that's me."
Crowd: *That's me.*

I come from the kind of ground
that cracks you open
before it teaches you how to grow.
And still
I stand.
(*Pause—look up*)
If you're still standing after what tried to take you
say "I'm here."
Crowd: *I'm here.*

They tried to drown my story once.
Water filling lungs.
Fear filling memory.
I learned what it feels like
to wake up surrounded by strangers
and look for someone who is already gone.
(*Beat*)
If you've ever lost someone
and had to keep breathing anyway
say "I breathe."
Crowd: *I breathe.*

They called it an accident.
I called it unfinished.
Because trauma doesn't end
when the sirens stop
it follows you home,

sits beside your bed,
waits for night
to remind you what it still owns.
If your past ever knocked on your door at midnight
say "not today."
Crowd: *Not today.*

But hear me
I am not the nightmare.
I am the one who woke up.
(*Point to yourself, then the crowd*)
If you woke up and chose healing anyway
say "I woke up."
Crowd: *I woke up.*

I learned how to move like Earth
quiet, patient, grounded.
Not rushing healing.
Not explaining pain.
Just standing long enough
for truth to settle.
If you're learning to move at your own pace
say "my time."
Crowd: *My time.*

I learned that Fire can warm
or it can destroy
and not everybody holding a flame
is trying to light the way.
(*Pause—lower voice*)
If you've ever been burned by someone
who said they loved the craft
say "I see it."
Crowd: *I see it.*

Some people burn rooms
and call it art.
But me?

I learned restraint.
I learned breath.
I learned that survival is an intelligence
passed down through bones.
If your ancestors taught you how to endure
say "thank you."
Crowd: *Thank you.*

I learned that being soft
doesn't mean being breakable.
And being quiet
doesn't mean I forgot.
If softness saved you
say "still soft."
Crowd: *Still soft.*

So when they ask
why I speak the way I do,
why my words land heavy,
why my voice sounds like memory
tell them:
I come from a place
where living was an act of rebellion.
(*Let this breathe*)
If living itself was your resistance
say "I resist."
Crowd: *I resist.*

I am still here
not because it was easy
but because my instincts loved me enough
to keep me alive
until my voice caught up.
And tonight
(*Step closer to the mic*)
I speak
not for applause,
not for money,

not for validation
But because standing here
means the nightmare didn't win.
(*Final pause*)
Say it with me
I did.
Crowd: *I did.*

Second Round Poem — "Receipts"

I didn't come to make you comfortable.
I came to tell the truth
that keeps getting buried under hashtags
and candlelight.

See
we love dead poets
more than living whistleblowers.

We clap louder for bodies
than for warnings.

I watched a room turn into a crime scene
and then turn back into a business model.
New flyers.
Bigger prizes.
Same silence.

Tell me
how much is a life worth tonight?
Because first place says fifteen thousand
and second place says ten
and third place still gets five
but the truth?

The truth never makes the list.

We call it an isolated incident
when it fits our narrative.

We call it tragedy
when accountability feels too heavy.
We call it "art"
when harm wears a familiar face.
And don't misunderstand me
I love poetry.
But poetry has been used as cover
more times than we want to admit.

Open mics became open doors.
Safe spaces became transit points.
And everybody keeps asking
"Who pulled the trigger?"
When the real question is
who opened the room?

Who watched?
Who knew?
Who kept quiet because exposure
doesn't come with a cash prize?

We say "the system failed,"
but the system is fed
by our compliance.

By our silence.
By our refusal to look at the artist
and ask what they're really transporting.

Some of you confuse radical with righteous.
Some of you confuse volume with truth.
Some of you confuse a mic
with a moral compass.

And let me be clear
everybody screaming "justice"
after the blood dries
does not make you innocent.

Especially if you ignored the smoke
when Fire was still speaking.

I heard her.
She said people were disappearing.
She said art spaces were being used.
She said danger doesn't always look violent
sometimes it looks charismatic.

And we called her dramatic.
Then we called her missing.

Now we call it a cold case.

Cold cases don't mean unanswered.
They mean inconvenient.

They mean truth costs too much
and nobody wants to pay.
So if this poem makes you uneasy
good.

That's what accountability feels like
before it turns into change.
I'm not here to win your applause.
I'm here to remind you

Revolution doesn't sound pretty.
Truth doesn't rhyme clean.
And safety doesn't exist
where profit comes first.

This isn't just poetry.
It's a receipt.

And somebody in this room
knows exactly
what I'm talking about.

Third Round Poem — "All Four Directions"

I learned survival from **Water**
how to hold memory
without drowning in it.
How to let tears fall
without letting them erase me.
Water taught me
that what you try to bury
always finds its way back to the surface.

I learned truth from **Fire**
how it exposes before it comforts,
how it doesn't ask permission
to be seen.
Fire taught me
that silence feeds monsters
and light makes liars nervous.

I learned stability from **Earth**
how to stay when everything says run,
how to root myself
in a world that keeps shaking.
Earth taught me
that standing your ground
is an act of resistance.

And I learned freedom from **Wind**
how to speak even when my voice trembles,
how to move truth
from chest to mouth to room.
Wind taught me
that breath is power
and power multiplies when shared.

Tonight
I am all four.

I am Water remembering what was done.
I am Fire naming what they tried to hide.
I am Earth refusing to be moved by fear.
I am Wind carrying this truth
past the doors of this room.

You can't drown me
I learned how to swim.
You can't burn me
I learned how to control flame.
You can't bury me
I learned how to grow through concrete.
And you can't silence me
because the wind always finds a way in.

This is not a poem.
This is a direction.

North—where we remember.
South—where we heal.
East—where we rise.
West—where we release.
I am standing at the center
calling all of it home.

And if you feel unsettled
good.

That means the elements are working.

Because when Water, Fire, Earth, and Wind
agree on the truth
nothing stays buried.

(*Step back. Breathe. Let silence fall.*)

After the Applause

The noise lingered even after the lights came back up.

Not clapping—conversation.

Low, excited, charged.

Amelia stepped off the stage and found Laura first. Laura didn't say anything right away. She just hugged her long and grounding, the kind of embrace that doesn't rush a moment into explanation.

"That wasn't just winning," Laura finally said. "That was testimony."

Wyatt joined them, eyes still bright, a little stunned in the best way. "You didn't perform," he said carefully, like he didn't want to cheapen it. "You claimed the room."

They found a quiet corner away from the crowd. Amelia sat, hands still buzzing, breath finally slowing. The check felt unreal in her bag, but the win wasn't what stayed with her.

It was the silence after the last line.

The way the room listened.

The way people sat with it.

Laura spoke about the intention behind the poems how every word felt deliberate, like it had lived somewhere before it reached the mic. "You didn't waste a breath," she said. "You honored the space. You honored the people who didn't make it out."

Wyatt nodded. "There was meaning in it," he added. "Not shock. Not spectacle. Meaning. That's rare."

Amelia smiled, small and tired and full all at once. She told them she hadn't come to win. She came to speak honestly. To finish something. To let the elements move through her without forcing them into applause.

"And that's why it worked," Laura said. "Because it was rooted."

They sat there a little longer, letting the night settle around them. The venue buzzed on, already moving toward the next thing. But for Amelia, the moment felt complete.

She hadn't just returned to the mic.

She had returned to herself.

And this time, she didn't have to do it alone.

They stayed there longer than they planned.

Long enough for the crowd to thin out. Long enough for the adrenaline to soften into something quieter something earned. Amelia leaned back in her chair, finally letting the weight of the night settle into her body. Her shoulders dropped. Her hands stopped trembling.

Laura watched her closely. "I saw people crying," she said. "Not performative tears. The kind that come when something unlocks." She paused. "You gave people permission tonight. That's power."

Wyatt nodded, thoughtful. "What struck me," he said, "was how balanced it was. You didn't rage just to rage. You didn't mourn just to mourn. You moved through all of it memory, truth, grounding, breath and brought us with you." He smiled. "That's leadership, whether you call it that or not."

Amelia looked down at her hands, turning the moment over gently. "I wasn't trying to prove anything," she said. "I just needed to tell it honestly. With intention. No shortcuts." She exhaled. "I think that's why it landed."

Laura reached across the table and squeezed her hand. "You honored the people who couldn't speak. And you protected the ones who still can." Her voice softened. "That matters."

They talked about the poem's specific lines, pauses, the way silence had done as much work as sound. Laura mentioned the grounding, how the Earth imagery steadied the room when the Fire got hot. Wyatt talked about the Wind how Amelia's breath guided the audience, how the Water carried memory without drowning the message.

"It felt complete," he said. "Like a circle."

Amelia felt a warmth spread through her chest. Not pride alignment. The kind that comes when your inner compass finally points in the same direction as your actions.

Outside, the city hummed on. Inside, something had been set down.

As they stood to leave, Laura said it simply: "Whatever comes next, remember this you didn't just win a slam. You showed what poetry is for."

Wyatt held the door open. "And you didn't do it alone," he added. "You don't have too anymore."

Amelia stepped into the night with them beside her, grounded and clear. The applause had faded, the checks would be cashed, the flyers would change but the intention would stay.

She had spoken.

She had listened.

She had been witnessed.

And for the first time in a long time, that felt like enough

Amelia Awakened

Amelia awakened in a cold sweat, her sheets clinging to her skin as if they, too, had tried to hold her down. Her chest rose and fell sharply, breath uneven, shallow—like she had just run for her life and didn't know where she had ended up.

The nightmare had returned.

Bright lights.

All white.

A voice that wasn't loving but demanded belief.

Her body trembled as she sat up, pressing her feet into the floor to remind herself where she was. Home. Safe. Or at least that's what she whispered aloud, hoping the words would anchor her. Her heart raced as if it hadn't gotten the message yet.

This dream never came gently.

It always arrived soaked in fear, dripping from her pores, dragging the past back into the present. She could still hear the voice calm, commanding, absolute echoing in the corners of her mind long after she had woken up.

Do what I say or there will be death.

Amelia wiped her face with trembling hands, realizing she was drenched, as if she had been pulled from deep water instead of sleep. She swung her legs over the bed, grounding herself, counting her breaths the way she had learned to survive.

One.

Two.

Three.

The room was dark now, quiet, but her mind wasn't. Nightmares had a way of reopening doors she worked hard to keep shut reminding her that some wounds didn't announce themselves as pain. They disguised themselves as authority. As faith. As love.

She stood and walked to the mirror, studying her reflection. Wide eyes. Bare shoulders. A woman who had survived more than she ever said out loud.

"This isn't real," she whispered not to the dream, but to herself.

Still, she knew the truth:

Recurring nightmares were messages the body refused to forget.

And Amelia's spirit was asking to be heard.

She turned away from the mirror, wrapped herself in a blanket, and sat in the quiet listening to her breath slow, to her heartbeat steady.

Morning would come.

But tonight, she stayed awake.

Because some awakenings don't happen in daylight.

They happen in the dark, when the soul finally demands attention.

Awakened (The Nightmare)

I awoke to bright lights—too white, too clean—like the world had been scrubbed of shadows and sin. The room hummed softly, sterile and endless, with no corners to hide in. My body was dressed in all white, fabric loose against my skin, as if I'd been prepared for judgment or rebirth. I couldn't remember choosing this.

The lights flickered once.

Then he stepped forward.

He wore white too, but his was pressed sharp, deliberate. His feet made no sound on the floor. His eyes—dark, unwavering—locked onto mine like they'd been waiting centuries just for this moment.

"I'm Jesus in the flesh," he said calmly, as if stating the weather.

"And if you don't do what I say, there will be death."

The words didn't echo. They didn't need to. They sank straight into my chest.

I tried to speak, but my throat tightened. Something about him felt wrong—not loud, not angry—worse. Certain. The kind of certainty that doesn't ask questions, only obedience.

Behind him, others stood in rows, also dressed in white. Silent. Still. Their eyes were empty, like they'd already surrendered something precious and didn't remember what it was.

I realized then: this wasn't heaven.

It was a test of belief—how easily fear could be dressed up as faith, how quickly power could borrow holy language and call itself divine.

My heart pounded as the lights grew brighter, almost blinding.

And in that moment, I understood:

Not every voice that claims to be God comes with love.

Some come with control.

Some come wrapped in light, carrying darkness underneath.

And waking up—truly waking up—meant choosing to see.

Even if it cost everything.

Amelia's Prayer

God,
It's me again.
The quiet version of me.
The one who speaks when the world finally goes still.

I don't always know the right words,
but You've heard my silence before,
so I trust you'll understand this too.

I ask for protection
not just from what walks behind me in the dark,
but from the memories that chase me
when I'm standing in the light.

Teach my intuition to speak louder than my fear.
When something feels off, let me listen without apology.
When my body remembers what my mouth won't say,
help me honor that knowing.

Cover me when I walk alone.
Cover my car, my keys, my phone calls sent "just in case."
Cover the version of me that learned survival too early
and still flinches out of habit.

Help me trust again
not blindly,
but wisely.
Let discernment be my companion,
not paranoia.

If danger is near, move it away from me.
And if I must pass through it,
walk so close that fear forgets my name.

Remind me that I am not weak for being cautious,
that softness and strength can share the same body,
that I am allowed to take up space
and still choose safety.

Tonight, I ask for rest.
Real rest.
The kind where my shoulders drop
and my breath doesn't race ahead of me.

Hold me while I sleep.
Stand guard where I can't.
And when morning comes,
let me wake knowing I survived again
not by accident,
but by grace.

Amen.

When Wind Speaks

I got more stories to tell
some whispered,
some screamed,
some wrapped in make-believe
so the truth could breathe
without breaking me.

These stories lived in **Water** first.
Water held my tears, my memories, my dreams
that drifted in and out like tides.
It taught me how to feel
how to remember without drowning,
how to let emotion move instead of trap me beneath the surface.

Then came **Fire**.
Fire carried my anger, my voice, my need to be seen and heard.
It burned through silence, exposed lies, and demanded truth.
Fire taught me that rage could be a signal, not a sentence
that heat could forge clarity instead of destruction.

Earth followed.
Heavy. Solid. Unavoidable.
Earth was survival.
It was the tail the part of the story that drags behind you
but proves you lived through it.
Earth taught me how to stand, how to root myself in reality,
how to keep going even when the ground felt unforgiving.
It reminded me that scars are evidence of endurance.

And then… there was **Wind**.

Wind didn't arrive loud.
It arrived knowing.

Wind moved through the water and calmed the waves,
not by force, but by rhythm.

Wind reminded the water it didn't have to carry everything at once.

Wind touched the fire and softened the flames,
not extinguishing passion,
but cooling destruction
turning rage into breath,
truth into release.

Wind settled the earth,
lifting the dust, clearing the weight,
loosening what had been packed too tight for too long.

Wind whispered, *You can rest now. You've held enough.*

Wind is where I learned
that healing doesn't always come from holding on
sometimes it comes from letting move
what was never meant to stay.

This is where my stories meet.

Where water flows without fear,
fire burns with purpose,
earth stands without burden,
and wind carries what no longer needs to be carried.

I got more stories to tell
some lies, some truth, some make-believe
because imagination saved me when reality was too heavy,
and honesty freed me when silence tried to keep me small.

This is not the end.
This is the breath between chapters.
The pause before the next story rises.

And now...
I let the wind take it from here.

•••

Amelia depended heavily on her faith.

After she prayed, she felt steady enough to move through the morning. She called Laura to carpool for work, grateful for the familiar routine, then checked her phone—something she did instinctively, almost reverently.

Every morning, without fail, Kingston sent her a message.

Sometimes it was a single line.

Sometimes a blessing.

Sometimes a poem.

That morning, it was a poem.

She read it slowly, letting each word settle into her chest like calm water finding its level. His words always arrived like the tide—gentle, certain, returning when she needed grounding the most.

Tide
From Kingston

You are the shoreline
and I am the tide that keeps returning,
drawn by gravity I don't question.

I rise over you slowly,
palms pressing into heat and breath,
finding my balance in the rhythm we make together.

Water remembers water.
Every movement answers another
a language of sway and pull,
of bodies listening instead of speaking.

There is a music between us,
soft thunder under skin,
a build that rolls and gathers
until the waves forget where they end.

I open to you like the sea opens to the moon,
needing the depth only you know how to give,
wanting us tangled in the same current,
no separation only motion.

And when it breaks,
it breaks everywhere
a spilling of warmth and light,
a quiet after the storm
where we float,
full, connected,
still breathing each other in.

•••

Amelia closed her eyes after reading it.

She didn't rush to respond.

The poem didn't feel like desire alone it felt like recognition. Like being seen without having to explain herself. Like water being met by water, not questioned, not forced just understood.

She exhaled slowly.

The wind outside brushed against the window, soft and deliberate, as if agreeing.

For the first time that morning, Amelia felt calm enough to move forward not carried by fear, but guided by faith, connection, and the quiet certainty that she was not navigating life alone.

Amelia stared at the screen for a moment longer than usual. Kingston's words still lingered in her body, like water refusing to evaporate. She could feel the echo of them steady, rhythmic, undeniable.

She didn't overthink it.

She trusted the pull.

Her thumbs moved slowly, deliberately, as if she were answering more than a text answering a current that had already found her.

She sent him a poem.

When It Rains, It Pours
From Amelia

It begins with a tremor in the air
a hush before surrender.
The sky pulls close,
and the first drop lands like a breath
you didn't know you were holding.

Love arrives this way,
uninvited,
unapologetic.
It moves across skin,
slow as heat,
careful as worship.

Raindrops trace the curve of your neck,
sliding into the space
where pulse meets memory.
Every touch becomes a question
how much can you feel
before it consumes you?

The storm builds.
Bodies hum with thunder.
Lips part like clouds before lightning.
You can taste the sky in this kind of wanting
metallic, wild, endless.

Water gathers at your feet,
but you don't move.
You stand in it,
letting it claim you,
letting it strip everything false.

This is not the gentle kind of love.
This is flood.
This is surrender.
This is what it means
to be touched
and undone
in the same breath.

•••

After she hit send, Amelia rested the phone against her chest.
Her heart wasn't racing it was **listening**.
Outside, the morning wind stirred, lifting the heaviness just enough to remind her:
Water could be deep without drowning.
Fire could warm without burning.
Earth could hold without trapping.
And Wind
Wind knew when to move things forward.
She smiled softly, whispered a quiet thank-you under her breath, and stood up ready for the day, carried not by fear, but by faith, poetry, and the courage to be felt.
Laura texted Amelia saying she wasn't going to work that day because she wasn't feeling well and told her not to come to her house to pick her up. Amelia stared at the message, confused. That was strange Laura was never so brief or dismissive. Before Amelia could call her to ask what was wrong, her phone rang.
"Laura?" Amelia answered.
Laura's voice was barely a whisper. She reminded Amelia about the man in the dark clothing the one Amelia had noticed earlier. Amelia felt her chest tighten as Laura said he was next door, standing at her neighbor's door, knocking. Suddenly, the line filled with screams. Then a loud bang. Then more gunshots, sharp and terrifying, blaring through the phone.

Amelia screamed Laura's name, her heart racing, panic flooding her body. Sirens wailed in the background, and through the chaos Laura cried that she was still there, still alive.

When it rains, it pours. As Amelia begged Laura not to hang up, another call came in. She ignored it at first, but the caller was persistent. Her hands shaking, Amelia clicked over to answer while pleading with Laura to stay on the line. When she said hello, all she heard was sobbing. It was her twin sister. Through broken breaths, she told Amelia that Patricia had passed away. Amelia felt everything go numb. There were no words, no tears, no emotion she could reach. Finally, she spoke softly, telling her sister she was sorry for her loss, that she would be there if she was needed, and that she would call her later. They hung up.

Laura agreed to drive her car to work, and they arrived at the same time. Laura rushed over to Amelia's car, shaken and pale, and told her the neighbor was gone that he had taken her life. Yellow police tape stretched across the area, officers everywhere. Amelia pulled Laura into a tight hug, holding her as her body trembled. Laura then went inside to the restroom to wash her face, to try to steady herself, before they both went to work.

The phones rang nonstop, voices overlapping, time moving forward even though Amelia felt frozen. By lunchtime, they stepped outside together and finally talked through the events of the morning the screams, the sirens, the shock of it all. So much tragedy had happened before noon. Amelia briefly mentioned her mother's passing, admitting she felt numb and didn't want to talk about it. Laura respected her wishes without pressing.

When they returned to work, the building felt unusually quiet too quiet. As they walked in, they noticed their boss's office door standing open. Inside, their boss was slumped over, blood everywhere, a gunshot wound to the head. They didn't stop to process it. They ran out the door, away from the horror, hearts pounding with fear and disbelief. This day couldn't get any worse. Death felt like it was following them, and Amelia couldn't shake the saying that tragedies come in threes.

The detectives questioned them for hours. The same questions, over and over, circling back on themselves where were you standing, who did you see last, did you hear anything unusual, did you notice anyone suspicious. Time lost meaning under the fluorescent lights. Amelia and Laura repeated their answers until their voices cracked, until exhaustion settled into their bones. By the time they were finally released, it was nearly 3 a.m. Outside, the air was cold and empty, the city eerily quiet, as if it had already moved on from the violence that refused to loosen its grip on them.

The months that followed never fully settled. Life resumed on the surface work, errands, conversations but something underneath stayed tight, watchful. They still went out together, still walked each other to their cars, still checked their mirrors more than necessary. One night, driving home on the freeway, Laura noticed headlights behind them too close, too steady. The car stayed with them as Laura changed lanes, then sped up. The other car sped up too. Her heart began to pound as the distance between them disappeared, the engine screaming as both vehicles pushed faster, weaving through traffic, fear rising with every mile.

Suddenly, Laura's car jerked and stalled, stuck in the middle of the road like it had been chosen. Before she could even scream, the other car pulled up beside them. The driver's door flew open. A man moved fast too fast. The window shattered. Hands reached in, grabbing Amelia. She barely had time to cry out before she was dragged from the seat. Laura's screams tore through the night as Amelia was shoved into the trunk, the lid slamming shut, plunging her into darkness. The car sped away, leaving Laura hysterical on the freeway, screaming Amelia's name into the empty air.

Amelia woke to suffocating blackness. No light. No space. Just tight walls pressing in around her. The air felt thick, heavy, impossible to pull into her lungs. She gasped, her chest burning, fingers clawing at the surface around her, realizing she was trapped inside a box. Panic surged as her breaths grew shorter, her heartbeat thundered in her ears, and the darkness closed in completely.

Amelia heard people crying. The sound drifted through the darkness, muffled but unmistakable. Voices layered over one another grief, panic, disbelief. One voice cut through the rest, sobbing louder than the others, screaming, *"Not my sister!"* Amelia's chest tightened. That voice belonged to her twin. Terror settled deep in her bones as the truth formed in her mind with horrifying clarity. *I've been buried alive.* The thought echoed as she whispered a desperate prayer into the dark. *God, please help me.* Images flashed without order the ocean's symmetry, clear skies, laughter, moments of peace everything she had lived and loved collapsing into a blur.

She realized then that she had been buried her whole life in different ways conflicted, restricted, out of touch. Her heart pounded wildly, rhythmically contracting at nearly a hundred beats a minute, reminding her she was still here, still alive. A body capable of creating life, of multiplying love, while she felt her own slipping away. Her mind raced, prayers spilling out silently, but no one heard her. Dirt pressed down from above, heavy and final, clumps sealing her into the earth. *This can't be the end*, she thought. *I have unfinished things. Stories still inside me.* Somewhere beyond the darkness, light was calling.

But she didn't want to go. Not yet. There were too many untold stories, too much left unsaid. She fought to hold on, to stay strong until the very end, even as the same words repeated in her mind conflicted, restricted, out of touch mourning everything she felt she had missed. *I need you,* she pleaded silently. *Please don't let this be the end. This is not my time.*

A tingling crept into her fingertips. Her eyes flew open in the darkness. *I'm still alive.* But her body wouldn't respond. She couldn't move. She couldn't breathe. Panic surged as she heard a voice say softly, "It's time." Then came the click-clack of metal, the sound of chains rolling, the slow, deliberate lowering of her body deeper into the grave. Voices chanted above her *from ashes to ashes, dust to dust.* Someone said they were laying their loved one to rest. Someone said she did her best.

Inside the box, Amelia screamed without sound. *I lived my life without fear or regret*, she told herself desperately. *But this is not the time for me to rest.*

The earth will not be my resting place.

It is too early.

I have too much to live for.

The weight above me presses down, but I refuse to surrender to it. I refuse to let soil and silence decide my ending. My breath is shallow, my body trapped, yet my spirit is loud—louder than the dirt, louder than the prayers spoken too soon. I am not done loving. I am not done telling stories. I am not done becoming who I was meant to be.

This darkness is not peace.

This stillness is not rest.

I have laughter left in me, tears that still need meaning, words that have not yet found their way onto the page. I have faith that has carried me this far, and it will not abandon me now. The earth may try to claim me, but it does not get the final word.

Not today.

Not like this.

I press my will against the silence and hold on to the smallest spark of air, the faintest pulse of life, trusting that somewhere above, something—or someone—is moving toward me. Because I am still here. I am still fighting. And this story is not finished.

Amelia could feel the wind against her skin, cool and insistent, slipping through the cracks like a promise that she was not alone. It moved over her gently, urging her to breathe, to stay present, to remember that even buried, air still finds its way in. The wind whispered to her spirit, not yet, lifting the panic just enough for her to hold on.

She felt fire next deep in her chest, in the place where fear turns into will. It pulled at her, demanding that she fight, that she refuse to surrender. Fire reminded her that survival lives in action, that strength is sometimes loud, sometimes violent, but always necessary. It told her to save herself.

Then water rose within her memory, steady and powerful. It reminded her of every wave she had already survived, every storm she had moved through and come out breathing on the other side. Water did not panic it endured. It taught her that strength could be fluid, that even in tight spaces, she could adapt, push, and persist.

Wind steadied her breath.

Fire fueled her will.

Water carried her strength.

And somewhere beneath the weight of the earth, Amelia understood this was not where her story ended.

Through the muffled weight of earth and silence, Amelia heard her sister's voice faint at first, then sharp with urgency.

The truth didn't come all at once—it slammed into me in flashes. I was tired of living in her shadow. Everything was always about her, about control, about watching my every move until I no longer felt like my own person. It was exhausting. When I got pregnant and chose to follow through with the pregnancy—when I had twins—something in her snapped. She was flustered, devastated, unraveling right in front of me. I didn't understand it then, but now, buried beneath layers of dirt and silence, it's all coming back.

This crazy, narcissistic, envious rage—*she* was the one who kidnapped me. *She* buried me alive. The realization hits harder than the weight on my chest. Flashbacks come in and out as I drift in and out of consciousness. I hear her pacing above me, back and forth, mumbling words to herself, screaming, crying, arguing with voices only she can hear. I feel the ground shake when she stops, when she kneels, when she presses her hands into the earth like she's trying to decide if I'm still worth saving or finishing.

I can't breathe. Dirt fills my mouth when I gasp. My body is weak, but my mind is wide awake now. I plead with God in broken whispers no one can hear. *Please don't let this be the end. I have so much to live for.* Above me, she's still there, trying to figure out her next move. I can feel it her hesitation, her fear, her need to control what happens next. She hasn't left. Not yet. And as the earth tightens around me and my heartbeat grows louder in my ears, one terrifying truth settles in: my twin sister hasn't decided if she's done with me... and I'm still alive beneath her feet.

The truth doesn't scare me anymore it steadies me. Buried beneath the weight of the earth, I focus on what I can still feel. The ground is cold, heavy, real. I press my fingers into the dirt, anchoring myself, grounding my body the way I was taught *stay present, stay here.* I remind myself that the earth is not just a grave, it is also a place of holding. If it can carry the weight of my fear, maybe it can carry me too.

My thoughts slow, even as my heart races. I think of my children. I think of the life I fought for when I chose myself. I refuse to let this be the ending of my story. Above me, my sister is still pacing, still deciding, still tangled in her need to control what she can no longer own. But down here, in the darkness, I realize something she never understood I am rooted deeper than her rage. I have survived her shadow my entire life.

I breathe through the panic. I talk to the earth like it can hear me. *Hold me a little longer,* I whisper. *Not to keep me but to remind me I belong to myself.* My body is trapped, but my mind is no longer hers. And as the dirt settles and her footsteps fade just enough to leave uncertainty hanging in the air, one final thought grounds me completely:

This is not my end.

This is my becoming.

To be continued...

I Got More Stories To Tell, Tale, Tail

And Still I Speak Through Poetry

Three Shadows

Past. Present. Future.

The past…
is a weight on my chest
a collection of scars, hidden and loud,
they scream even when my mouth is still.

Questions hang heavy, unanswered
and every step forward,
it pulls me back like I'm tied to
pain I don't remember but can't forget.

I carried so much
resentment,
sorrow,
anger,
I wore them like armor,
too tired to take them off,
too broken to leave them behind.
I ran from myself.
The hurt was all I knew.

But the present…
is a soft quiet fight,
a tenderness to the anger,
a learning that I was never broken,
just bruised,
just caught in a storm I didn't understand.
I'm learning the rhythm of healing,
like a song I've forgotten but always knew.
Every breath is a small revolution
to sit with myself
without shame.
To forgive what once felt unforgivable
and love myself again,
like I'm new.

I am learning to trust my hands,
my heart,
to build from the ruins,
piece by piece,
with care.

And the future?
It is a promise I've just started to make.
Not perfect,
but whole.
The shadows will still come,
the echoes of who I was,
but I will face them,
not as the girl I used to be,
but as the woman I'm becoming.
I'll know how to hold my pain
without letting it own me.
I'll remember my worth,
no longer a question,
but a truth I walk in.
I'll love all of me—
even the parts that are still healing.
I'll trust in the path
because I know it leads to me,
to the whole of me,
and I'm ready to be all that I am.

Three shadows,
but each one is part of me,
and I hold them all
with love.

My Story to Tell

You can write your false statements,
pretend you know my story,
my life, my pain,

my struggles, my journey
but you have never walked a day in my shoes.

My shoes don't fit your feet.
Get your own.
I am the author of my life,
this journey,
this story.
No matter the pain,
no matter the struggle
plot twist: I win in the end.

Paint me however you like.
Label me.
Judge me.
Twist the story.

But know this:
my heart is pure.
my loyalty is rare.
my intentions are real.

I stand firm in who I am,
with or without your approval.
I know my worth,
and I'm not afraid
to sit alone.

Because my solitude is sacred,
my voice is power,
my truth is unshakable,
and my story
is mine to tell.

I learned how to listen for footsteps.
How to read moods the way other kids read books.
How to stay alert, even in my dreams.
Sleep didn't come gently it came in pieces.

Short. Broken. Guarded.
And when it did, nightmares followed
replaying memories I never invited back.
I woke up tired, already exhausted
from surviving something that was supposed to be over.
It wasn't until my late twenties
that safety stopped feeling like a rumor.
That my body slowly began to believe
what my mind was trying to tell it.
That the doors were locked.
That no one was coming to hurt me.
That rest was allowed.
Even now, some days my heart still races.
Not because I'm in danger
but because it remembers a time when I always was.
And I remind it, softly, patiently:
We made it.
We are here.
You can slow down now.

If I Awaken in Los Angeles
A Love Letter to the City That Still Believes in Dreams

When I was born in Los Angeles, I do not rise alone.

I rise with the palms that stretch like giants reaching for the sun,

with the sirens and the silence,

the traffic and the poetry,

the grit and the glitter living side by side.

This city is a heartbeat—steady, loud, and unashamed.

A place where every sidewalk crack has a story,

every mural is a love note,

every stranger is a question mark waiting to become a sentence.

Los Angeles does not introduce itself slowly.

It grabs you by the soul and whispers,

"Who are you becoming?"

Because here, identity is not fixed

it is painted, reinvented, broken down, rebuilt, renamed.

I have seen this city cradle the lost and crown the found.

I've watched dreamers walk into auditions, shelters, classrooms, and open mics

hoping for a yes

and I've watched them learn to survive the no.

LA teaches you: the only thing stronger than struggle

is the one who still wakes up the next morning.

If I awaken in Los Angeles,

I awaken in the middle of possibility,

in a mosaic of cultures, colors, languages, neighborhoods, recipes, rhythms, and prayers.

A city where tamales taste like gospel

where the ocean baptizes the tired

and the mountains remind us we were never meant to stay small.

This is a city of contradictions

where homelessness and Hollywood share the same sky

where wealth can live across the street from wounds

where sunshine doesn't mean safety

but hope still shows up every day anyway.

And yet

Los Angeles loves us without apology.

She gives us sunsets so dramatic they feel personal

street performers who sing like they're saving the world

neighbors who water the sidewalk just to cool the day

old men playing chess outside donut shops,

artists making futures out of recycled dreams.

If I awaken in Los Angeles, I awaken knowing

this city is not just where I live

it is a mirror.

A reminder that healing is not quiet

success is not simple

love is not tidy

and growth is not always gentle.

Here, we learn to create ourselves out of the pieces that survived.

Here, we remember that even concrete can bloom.

Here, we understand that belonging is not found

it is built.

So I say this with all my chest:

Dear Los Angeles

thank you for the lessons wrapped in palm trees,

the sunsets that refuse to repeat themselves

the strangers who feel like future friends

and the way you hold both pain and possibility in the same palm.

If I awaken in Los Angeles,

I awaken in a city that demands I rise

that dares me to dream louder

that teaches me love is work

but worth it.

And I will love you back,

not for who you pretend to be

but for who you are

an unfinished masterpiece

still shaping the people who dare to call you home.

Heart Racing

My heart learned how to run before I learned how to rest.

It raced through hallways of uncertainty, through nights that never felt quiet, through days that asked too much of a child who only wanted to feel safe.

Fear wasn't an emotion it was a location. I lived there.

Every tomorrow felt like a question mark leaning toward danger. I never knew what I was waking up to, or if sleep itself would betray me. There was no safe place to land, no corner of the world that whispered you're okay now.

Nighttime was the worst.

That's when my body remembered

everything my mouth couldn't say.

The aches.

The bruises that lived under skin and silence.

The emotional wounds that never showed but screamed the loudest.

Even when the house was still, my chest wasn't.

My heartbeat like it was being chased.

Like if it slowed down, something bad would catch up.

Who Am I?

I am someone who has lived through deep trauma and profound transformation.

I come from a dysfunctional family where love was never taught, hugs were never given, and emotional safety was never a part of my upbringing.

I grew up in survival mode, never truly knowing what love looked or felt like. Even now, I still struggle with hugs physical touch is something I'm slowly learning to embrace.

My journey hasn't been easy. I've endured losses that shook the very ground beneath me, including a near-death experience that changed everything. But even before that, I was already fighting through emotional storms carrying pain I never chose, yet somehow learning to rise from it stronger each time.

I spent years working in social services, sitting across from people with the same story over and over again searching for love, craving to be seen, held, and healed. That's when I realized: love isn't something you wait to receive. You have to find it in yourself first. And once you do, it becomes the foundation you build everything else on.

That's who I am a woman learning to love herself daily, and teaching others how to do the same.

Dear Little Lost Girl

I see you.

You were never loud about your pain.

You learned early how to shrink,

how to be quiet enough not to be noticed,

how to survive rooms that never felt safe.

You were not broken.

You were adapting.

I'm sorry I didn't protect you the way you deserved.

I'm sorry I made you grow up too fast,

carry weight meant for adults,

learn lessons through hurt instead of guidance.

You did the best you could with what you were given.

And I honor you for that.

To the Misplaced Teenager

You were angry and tender at the same time.

Confused about love.

Confused about your body, your voice, your worth.

You wore strength like armor

because softness felt dangerous.

You pretended not to care

because caring had cost you too much.

I'm sorry for the nights you cried alone,

for the questions no one answered,

for the times you thought something was wrong with you

instead of understanding something was wrong around you.

You were not too much.

You were simply unmet.

To the Young Adult Unlearning Pain

You tried to build a life

while still carrying wounds you never named.

You chased love, approval, stability

sometimes in places that mirrored your trauma.

I forgive you for the choices you made while hurting.

For the silence.

For the self-doubt.

For staying too long.

For leaving too fast.

You were learning without a map.

You were surviving and becoming at the same time.

And Now... To the Woman I Am Today

I welcome you.

You are softer, but stronger.

You listen to your body now.

You pause.

You breathe.

You choose yourself without apology.

You no longer confuse chaos with love

or pain with purpose.

You understand that healing is not linear,

and peace is allowed.

You carry the girl, the teen, and the young woman inside you

not as burdens,

but as proof of resilience.

This Is My Apology

I'm sorry it took me so long to love you out loud.

I'm sorry I didn't always choose you first.

I'm sorry I believed survival was the same as living.

But I am here now.

I am listening now.

I am loving you gently, intentionally, fully.

You are safe with me.

You are home.

I love you.

The Love of My City (Where I'm From)

Palm trees, blue skies
they say it never rains here.
Movie stars, flashy cars,
bright lights selling dreams
we don't always get to touch.

Gunshots echo between hope and sirens,
people leaving before their time,
names turned into numbers,
lives treated like footnotes.
To some, we don't matter
but we know better.

Family cookouts,
be in before the streetlights come on,
paper plates, loud laughter,
corner liquor stores and churches
sharing the same block.
East side, west side,
red, blue—lines drawn deep,
taught early, understood quick.

Educated in survival,
street smart by necessity.
Grandma passed
the glue came undone.
Single-parent homes,

roles reversed,
last names carrying weight
we didn't choose.

Kicked out too young,
no map, no manual,
just a moment of silence
for childhood cut short.
Teenage parents raising babies
while still learning themselves,
stress heavy in young hands.

Late nights, two jobs,
no car,
bus stops holding our secrets,
dreams folded into transfer tickets.

No real home,
trust misplaced,
alone and confused,
standing at the crossroads,
asking the city,
Which way do I choose?
Los Angeles,
is not just where I live
it is a mirror.
A reminder that healing is not quiet,
success is not simple,
love is not tidy,
and growth is not always gentle.

Here, we learn to create ourselves out of the pieces that survived.
Here, we remember that even concrete can bloom.
Here, we understand that belonging is not found
it is built.

So I say this with all my chest:
Dear Los Angeles

thank you for the lessons wrapped in palm trees,
for the sunsets that refuse to repeat themselves,
for the strangers who become family,
and the way you hold both pain and possibility in the same palm.

Los Angeles,
is a city that demands I rise,
that dares me to dream louder,
that teaches me love is work
but worth it.
And I will love you back
not for who you pretend to be,
but for who you are:
an unfinished masterpiece
still shaping the people who dare to call you home.
This is the love of my city
rough, honest, unfinished.
It raised me, tested me,
hurt me, held me.
And even with all its scars,
this is where I'm from,
and I carry it
everywhere I go.

Believing in Who I Am

I believe in who I am
not who I was told to be,
not who I had to become to survive,
but who I am when I stand in my truth.
I believe in my growth,
in the lessons that shaped me,
in the healing that continues to unfold.

Every scar carries wisdom.
Every step forward is earned.
I believe in my voice,

even when it trembles.
I believe in my purpose,
even when the path feels unclear.
I trust that who I am is enough right here, right now.

I no longer shrink to fit spaces that cannot hold me.
I no longer question my worth when I know my heart.
I honor my journey, my resilience, my becoming.

Believing in who I am
means choosing myself daily,
leading with love,
and standing firm in my values.

I am still growing.
I am still learning.
And I believe in me—fully, boldly, unapologetically.

I Played the Hand I Was Dealt

I played the hand I was dealt,
no reshuffle, no mercy, no pause in the game.
Cards slapped down early
loss, silence, survival
and I learned the rules by bleeding through them.

Some hands were heavy with history,
creased edges, names I didn't choose,
faces staring back at me like fate
asking, What you gonna do with this?

I didn't always win.
Sometimes I folded my pride.
Sometimes I bet on myself with nothing left.
Sometimes I had to put on my poker face,
bluff with one pair in my hand
and make it look like I was holding a royal flush.

I got next.

I learned how to read the room,
how to bluff fear,
how to stack patience when hope ran low,
how to turn a losing streak
into a lesson.

They thought the cards defined me.
Red or black.
Good or bad.
But they forgot the hands that hold them
have power too.

And what they never saw
what I never showed
I always had an ace in the hole.
Faith.
Instinct.
A quiet knowing that I survive
what should've broken me.

So I played the hand I was dealt
not perfectly,
not quietly,
but honestly.

I turned scars into strategy,
pain into placement,
memory into muscle.

And here's the truth they don't tell you about the game:
you don't have to change the cards
to change the outcome.

You just have to stay at the table
long enough
to learn your worth.

Because I played the hand I was dealt
with an ace in the hole,
poker face steady,
still standing,
still shuffling forward,
still alive enough
to deal myself a future.

To My Readers,

If you made it here, thank you. Thank you for sitting with the truth, the lies, and the in-between spaces where make-believe becomes survival. These stories were never meant to give you all the answers. They were meant to remind you that even in confusion, even in pain, there is meaning. There is movement. There is breath.

Some of what you read is real. Some of it is imagined. And some of it lives in that sacred place where memory, healing, and storytelling blur. That space is intentional. Because life doesn't come to us in straight lines it comes in fragments, in flashes, in tails we carry behind us and tales we're still brave enough to tell.

If any part of these pages made you pause, reflect, feel seen, or uncomfortable that's okay. Growth often lives there. I hope you found pieces of yourself in these stories or at least felt less alone in your own.

This is not an ending. It's a grounding. A breath before the next chapter. There are still more stories to tell mine, yours, and the ones we haven't yet found the courage to speak aloud.

Until then, stay present. Stay curious. Water your gifts, let that fire burn, Stay rooted in who you are becoming, and allow the wind to guide you.

With love and truth,
Coach A. Lee
I Got More Stories to Tell

Acknowledgments

This book is not just a collection of stories—it is a reflection of every voice, every moment, every experience that has shaped me along the way. And for that, I give thanks.

To my family—thank you for being my foundation. Through every high and low, every chapter of growth, every moment of doubt—you stood beside me. Your love, your patience, and your belief in me have carried me further than words can express.

To my friends—my circle, my tribe—thank you for encouraging me, listening to my ideas, laughing with me, growing with me, and reminding me of who I am when I needed it most. You've poured into me in ways that have helped me stay grounded and inspired.

To my creative community, Creative Love Network—this is home. Thank you for creating a space where expression is not only welcomed but celebrated. To every poet, artist, performer, and visionary within this network—you inspire me daily. You remind me that storytelling is power, and that our voices matter.

To every person in my social circle who has supported my creativity— whether you shared a post, came to a show, read my words, gave feedback, or simply believed in me—this book carries a piece of you. Your support does not go unnoticed.

To those who have challenged me—who pushed me, questioned me, and even doubted me—you, too, played a role in this journey. You helped me dig deeper, write harder, and become more intentional with my voice.

And finally, to you—the reader. Thank you for opening this book and allowing my stories to meet yours. Some of these pages may feel like truth, some like fiction, and some like something in between—but all of it is real in its own way.

Because at the end of it all...
We all have stories to tell.

What's yours?

About the Author

Coach A. Lee | Award-Winning Transformative Coach for Personal Growth, Healing, Health & Wellness

Chef • Poet • Author • Facilitator • Keynote Speaker
Los Angeles, California

Coach Andrea "A. Lee" Lee is a dynamic, award-winning, and multifaceted creative whose work lives at the intersection of healing, storytelling, emotional intelligence, and self-love. With over 20 years of experience in social services, she is a certified Life/Love & Relationship Coach, Emotional Intelligence Facilitator, Parenting Instructor, Case Manager, professional Chef, Poet, Author, and Spoken Word Artist dedicated to helping individuals reclaim their voice, power, and truth.

As a core leader within Creative Love Network and President of the Los Angeles Poet Society, Coach A. Lee has built transformative platforms that blend education with entertainment creating healing workshops, poetry showcases, community programs, and immersive experiences rooted in self-discovery, resilience, and emotional growth.

A three-time Pan African Film Festival featured spoken word artist and performer, and two-time host Presented by Diverse Verses LA, A. Lee is known for her commanding yet compassionate presence, emotional depth, and fearless storytelling. Her work invites audiences into the spaces we often avoid truth, trauma, love, survival, and rebirth while offering tools to heal and evolve. She is also a keynote speaker for the Los Angeles County Department of Children and Family Services (DCFS), where she speaks on self-love, emotional intelligence, resilience, healing, and community transformation.

Her literary work spans self-help, poetry, storytelling, and children's literature, including:

- *The Power to Change the Way You Love Yourself* (4-Book Series)
- *The Power to Change the Way You Love Yourself: 10 Life-Changing Steps to Self-Love- Work-Shop*
- *Expressions of Love: Feelings of Love, Courage & Betrayal*

- *Cooking with Little Chef Lee & The Culinary Kids* (Children's Culinary Series)
- *Connections Between Us*
- *I Got a Story to Tell, Tale, Tail*
- *I Got More Stories to Tell, Tale, Tail:*

Upcoming Works:
- *How I Found the Power to Change the Way I Love Myself: Her Story – My Journey*
- *Dear Black Man / Dear Black Woman: Voices in Unity*
- *The Power to Change The Way You Love — an ongoing Journey — Creating a Safe Space*

Through her writing, performances, workshops, and keynote addresses, Coach A. Lee creates space for reflection, grounding, and transformation reminding readers and audiences alike that healing is possible, stories matter, and survival deserves to be honored.

"Support Is Everything."
— Coach A. Lee

Stay Connected

To keep in touch and learn more about Coach A. Lee's work, books, workshops, and upcoming events, visit **www.AuthorAndreaLee.com**

For inquiries, bookings, or collaborations, email **Andrea@CreativeLoveNetwork.com**

Explore workshops, programs, and community experiences at **www.CreativeLoveNetwork.com**

Follow Coach A. Lee on social media:
Instagram: @Coach_A.Lee | @Ms.Drea_ThePoet
YouTube: Coach A. Lee | Creative Love Network
TikTok: I Got A Story to Tell, Tale, Tail | Coach A. Lee

Thank you for your continued support and for being part of the journey.

About the Publisher: Creative Love Network

Creative Love Network is a Southern California based poetry and live performance organization that utilizes spoken word and the arts as a means to entertain audiences, deliver targeted messages and positively impact communities. The company is rooted in the understanding that words, whether they are spoken, sang, read or heard, have the power to change lives and shape the world.

The Creative Love Network's Four Pillars — foundational company principles and affirmations — are:

Love:

I will love myself and others, and I will do things out of love.

Organize:

I will organize my life, and I will seek order over chaos.

Value:

I will value the whole of me, and I will see the value in others.

Evolve:

I will evolve into a better me, and I will always work to improve as a person.

I believe that when I LOVE, ORGANIZE, VALUE & EVOLVE,
I am doing my part to make the world a better place.

L.O.V.E.
CreativeLoveNetwork.com